NATIVE VOICES

A Literary Collection of Emerging Indigenous Writers

KINSMAN AVENUE PUBLISHING, INC.
www.kinsmanquarterly.org

© 2024 Kinsman Avenue Publishing, Inc.

Registered with the U.S. Library of Congress
Library of Congress Control Number: 2024940567

Printed in the United States of America

Native Voices: A Literary Collection of Emerging
Indigenous Writers

ISBN: 978-1-962121-08-8   Paperback
ISBN: 978-1-962121-09-5   eBook format

Cover Design by Anastasia Simone
Interior Book Design by Summer Greigh

Edited by Monique Franz
Co-Editors: Dawn Leas and Sandhya Barlaas
Poetry Editors: Dawn Leas and Odette Cortés
Supporting edits by Sophia Obianamma Ofuokwu, Mildred J Mills,
and Radiyah Nouman

Contributing authors in alphabetical order:
*Alysha Brooks, Brooke Waukau, Dr. Deidra Suwanee Dees, Joseph Marcel
Ikhenoba, Radiyah Nouman, Rizka Nafiah, Shantell Powell, Shrinidhi
Darbhe, Sophia Obianamma Ofuokwu, Sunday Abel, Tonnie MAC,
Vernica Goel*

NAT/VE
VOICES

A Literary Collection of Emerging Indigenous Writers

Edited by Monique Franz
Co-Editors: Dawn Leas & Sandhya Barlaas
Poetry Editors: Dawn Leas & Odette Cortés
Cover Design: Anastasia Simone

Dedicated to global Indigenous communities
as you recover what was taken and lost.

Editor's Note

In the quiet of a lecture hall, I sat listening to Pete Hill from the Native American Community Services of Erie and Niagara Counties, Inc. (NACS). The talk, titled "Supporting Native American Students—Discussions of Indigenous Cultures, Histories, and Dynamics," introduced the dark legacy of American Indian boarding schools—how these institutions stripped away culture, language, and self-esteem from countless Native American lives.

As Hill detailed these historical atrocities, I couldn't help but draw parallels to the generational trauma experienced by my own African American ancestors, but it also reminded me of my not-so-distant Native DNA.

Although I am not a registered Native American, my lineage, as is true of many African Americans, is deeply interwoven with the Indigenous fabric of this land. My great-great-great grandparents were Cherokee and Blackfoot natives, and my paternal grandfather was a "Bahamian Indian." I couldn't help but empathize with the stories, struggles, and endurance of Native Americans because their blood runs through my veins.

When we launched the Native Voices contest, we expected Indigenous authors from the Americas (and hoped to have submissions from Australia, New Zealand, and Polynesian communities), but we were pleasantly surprised to receive so many from Asia and Africa. We divided the book into the major parts of the world of those who submitted.

This anthology of Indigenous writers, poets, and playwrights is an endeavor to honor Indigenous heritage. It is a celebration and a remembrance, a means to contribute to the restoration of a culture, history, and identity that has endured unspeakable trials. Our sincerest gratitude to guest judge Tim Jones of the Seminole Tribe of Florida for his contribution to entry selections. These pages are not just filled with words; they are filled with the voices of resilience, the echoes of lost languages, and the strength of spirits unbroken by time.

— Monique Franz

VOICES OF ASIA

VOICES OF THE AMERICAS

VOICES OF AFRICA

Asia

Section

1

Away the Water Drains
Radiyah Nouman

A asiya shivered. Water dripped from her arms and face as she stood ankle-deep on the edge of the river. Her mother's bangles clinked a few feet away from where she stood.

Ching, ching, ching. They sounded lovely, jingling away as her Ami Jan performed her ablution. Aasiya glanced to where her grandmother stood hunched over with the other women, washing her feet. They stood deeper in the water, where little girls weren't allowed because of the strong waves.

A crisp winter breeze started up again, so cold that Aasiya was sure her nose would fall off. She clamped her hands on it. She couldn't be without a nose. Meanwhile, the water glistened and gushed, unaffected.

Dadi Ji called, "Aasiya *puttar*, if you're done, come inside with me."

The seven-year-old turned and sloshed over to the green shore where her *chappal* had been haphazardly placed. She pulled down the lowers of her *shalwar* from where she had tucked them around

1

her knees and hobbled over to the mud hut. Her grandmother was already feeding more wood to the sputtering flames. Aasiya knelt in front of it, letting the warmth seep in while keeping a close eye on her little sister Saima, who babbled away in a corner of the room. Saima had gotten her grubby hands on Aasiya's favourite toy one time. *Never again.*

Dadi Ji spread out the prayer mats in the time that Ami Jan came inside. The three of them stood, adjusting their headscarves before beginning their Friday prayers. Aasiya's headscarf was the best in her opinion. It was a light pink silk with blue flowers embroidered on it. The cloth was a gift from her father. He bought one for each of the girls out of the extra pay he got when the farm earned a profit from the harvest last year. Aasiya's older brother said it was due to 'soil fertility.' Older brother was eager to show off what he learned in school. Dadi Ji's headscarf was a rich brown with rust-red flowers, while Ami Jan had pink flowers on lush green. Saima hadn't yet been born.

They ended prayers and set about making lunch. Aasiya crouched down, rolling her sleeves as her mother placed a metal dish on the ground. Aasiya punched and rolled the mixture of flour and water until it formed a nice dough. She played with it until her mother scolded her and made her take it outside where Dadi Ji had trapped a small fire in a circle of stones, a flat pan already heating on top of it.

The two women, both young and old, separated the dough into 12 smaller pieces, and rolled each between the palms of their hands. Nice and thin. Dadi Ji slapped one onto the pan, using her fingers to flip it over once it was cooked through. Aasiya could only watch. Little girls weren't allowed near fires.

After roasting the *rotis*, the women spread out the few dishes on the worn-down carpet in the centre of the room. Ami Jan placed the curry in the middle, still in the *karahi* it cooked in.

2

"Amma! Ruqqia! We're home!" a familiar male voice called from outside.

"Oh good! I was beginning to worry. Come quick, or the food will get cold. Hassan, take off your shoes. How many times do I have to tell you?!" Ami Jan went full mother hen on her husband and son as they returned from work and school.

Aasiya ran to greet her *Abu*, who lifted her into his arms. She grinned at the grunt he released. She was getting bigger!

Saima screamed her head off, demanding the attention, which Aasiya's older brother duly supplied, screaming back at her. Dadi Ji calmly and expertly directed everyone back towards the food, simultaneously murmuring blessings on each of them.

The Bajwas all sat down to eat, having the river's music soothing their ears as it played its usual melodies.

***

Aasiya heaved her bucket out of the river, balancing it on her shoulder as she sloshed her way out of the water. She had to go further in to fill the bucket up, since the edge of the river had dried up over the years. If only it would rain. She liked the rain.

"Ami, here's the water," Aasiya said, turning to her mother, who sat on the bare floor, fanning herself with a handmade straw fan made by Hassan. Beads of sweat trickled down her forehead as the scorching July heat permeated every corner of the house.

"Give me a glassful of it, *beta*. I really cannot stand this heat any longer." Ami Jan's lip trembled. "Oh God, why do you punish me so?"

Aasiya sighed, exhausted from her mother's tantrums. Being 13 years old, even she wasn't that moody. Aasiya trudged off to do the remaining chores. She grabbed the soap and laundry and made her way back to the glistening river.

The rocks, once a part of the riverbed, were now exposed and smoothed from years of erosion. Aasiya vigorously scrubbed the clothes; good exercise to let out her teenage frustrations. As she washed and wrung them out in the river, she splashed water on herself. The sun blazed down, and she could almost feel her skin melting.

"Aasiya! Get the food ready, your brother will be back soon." Ami Jan called out from the doorway, stroking her round belly. "He'll be starving, poor child."

The river calmly whispered its secrets to the indifferent ears as Aasiya stomped over to the mud hut, crushing the dry grass beneath her. She wanted to sit down and fan herself. Frustration rolled off her in waves as she chopped and cooked the thick slab of meat given them the other day by Abu's employer.

"Oi, *chotti*! Make yourself useful for once." Aasiya harshly yanked Saima into the makeshift kitchen. "Knead this dough."

The little girl quickly sat to work at the sound of her sister's annoyance. However, she got a scolding after playing with the dough instead.

By the time lunch was ready, Dadi Ji hobbled back from visiting the neighbours, *chaddar* wrapped around her frail figure. Further off, Hassan came down the dirt path. Aasiya had half a mind to throw him in the water, sending that smug face floating downstream.

Hassan's arrival meant her mother and grandmother's attention would turn to him. They fussed over the beads of sweat on his forehead, offered him glasses of water, and stroked his hair. He basked in the glory. The two women asked him about his day, worrying over him working too hard.

Meanwhile, Aasiya rushed to get the dishes in place, sweating profusely. The sickly sweet, onion-like stench emanating from her armpits. She would need to take a wash for sure.

After lunch was done, Saima and Aasiya were tasked with cleaning the dishes. Dadi Ji offered to help, but her age was taking a physical toll. She couldn't exert herself for long and thus fell asleep on the charpoy in the shade of the jamun trees. Meanwhile, Ami Jan sewed a small baby-sized garment by hand. Hassan was no help, as usual.

When the dishes were done, Aasiya, unable to bear the stench any longer, grabbed the bucket from the tiny bathroom and made her way to the river. It no longer had strong currents, or maybe she was just old enough to be able to face them now. She had to go quite far in to fill the bucket. The coolness of the water, a relief—like being saved by a cool prince from a fiery hellhole.

Night settled in by the time Abu came home. He threw a stone in the water, blaming and cursing it for the lack of crop.

The river watched in silence.

***

"... because, of course, she's our daughter now. We worry for her reputation in the village. Besides, wearing a *burqa* is respectable in our religion," Nasreen Khala squeezed out before resuming her consumption of the *pakoras* and tea.

Ami Jan nodded, eye bags prominent as ever. Aasiya sat obediently in the room's corner, empty tea tray in hand. Outside, she could hear her father and brother chatting with Abdul. He was going on about his newest job in the factory; his fifth in two months. He claimed it was temporary, as he was destined to be the owner of a massive farm. Abu and Hassan agreed.

After the mother and son left, Aasiya cleared the dishes. Abu came inside with Hassan, the latter looking a little stony. She made herself scarce, predicting the conversation he would raise.

"Abu...," Hassan began.

Her father sighed before saying, "Beta, I know what you're going to say. We will find you a wife, I promise. But let us fulfill our responsibility with Aasiya first. She's sixteen. If she doesn't marry now, no one will want her, and she will be stuck in the house. Once she goes, we will find you someone too, I promise."

Hassan huffed, but went quiet. Aasiya knew he was frustrated that Abdul, his classmate, would marry first. Again, he was more focused on finding himself a wife than wishing for his sister's well-being in another house. In *her* house, as Ami Jan had drilled into her. Aasiya's home was no longer with her parents but with her future husband and mother-in-law.

Aasiya stepped outside for air. It scared her how rapidly everything happened. She was to be a wife, which also made her feel a little giggly. A lot of her friends had gotten married or were engaged. They often told Aasiya that she wouldn't understand their conversations since she was just a kid. Now, she was like them, finally an adult! Her mother told her she would find her *Shehzadah* or Prince Charming one day. Now her dreams were a reality.

Lost in her daydreams, Aasiya made her way to the graves by the riverside. Wildflowers grew over the four of them; two adult-sized, two infant-sized. Her two brothers never got a name, dying in childbirth. Her grandmother peacefully lay beside them, next to grandfather. The river gurgled, trickling down the vast plains. Spring was in full bloom.

Aasiya made her way over to the shallow water. The fish were long gone, and the river, a muddy, chemical-infused stream. Her hazy reflection sat in the rainbow circlets amidst the brown sediments. There she stood at the pinnacle of youth. A fresh round face, eyes darkened with *kajal*, a thick black braid. No wonder Abdul came running for her hand in marriage.

"Aasiya, come inside! Where's your *chaddar*?" Ami Jan yelled. She suddenly appeared, dragging her daughter towards the house, creating ripples in the water. "Be careful, you foolish girl. You're not a child anymore. You can't just step out without covering yourself."

"There's no one around!" Aasiya huffed. "It's not a big issue!"

"Everyone be damned. You are not to step foot out of the house without a *burqa* or a *chaddar* at the very least," she barked. "Did you not hear Nasreen Aapa? You must do as she and Abdul say, you hear me?"

The ripples spread along the water, disturbing its surface as the two women argued. The water struggled against itself.

Obedience. That was Aasiya's newest lesson for the next several weeks. Spring neared its end by the time they arranged her marriage date. It was earlier than expected, but her parents wanted her in her own place before summer.

In the days leading up to it, her mother drilled all kinds of lessons into her. *"Listen to your husband. Never raise your voice. Do the housework, help your mother-in-law. Don't complain. Be the backbone of the family. Never waiver."* Aasiya didn't believe it was as big a deal as her mother made it out to be.

When the day of the event came, it was chaos. Many *khalas*, the aunties, hovered over Aasiya, fretting over this and that. Women who had come for the ceremony cramped the tiny hut. The overwhelming mixture of scents in the air stung the eyes and made it difficult to breathe.

The older women tutted over Aasiya's clothes; each arranged to their own liking. They tugged at her hair, poked it with hairpins, and smeared bright red lipstick on her. The entire time, the chatter didn't falter. Each giving her readable looks.

Say goodbye to peace and quiet.
Life will never be the same again, girlie.
Best of luck. Childhood is over now.
Time to become a woman.

Aasiya fell into a daze as the heavy red *dupatta* was finally thrown over her. Nasreen Auntie patted her head and murmured in approval. Finally, after what felt like forever, the *Maulvi Sahab* was ushered in to lead the ceremony.

It felt like the world had paused. Suddenly, Aasiya felt scarily alone. All the women stared at her, waiting for her to say those two fateful words. Even her mother felt like a stranger. Instinctively, Aasiya tuned her ears to the soothing melody of the river.

She couldn't hear it.

"Qabool hai."

No rush of the water.

"Qabool hai."

No crash of the waves. Only the marital vows.

"Qabool hai."

Makeup-caked women offered her toothy congratulations. Her mother wiped tears and put on a smile. Food was passed around and inhaled. The main motive of the guests, accomplished.

Time passed in a whirl. Eventually, a thick *chaddar* was wrapped around Aasiya and she was led outside to where her family stood. Her family—her new husband and mother-in-law!

Women, who practically raised her in the small neighbourhood, wailed and wiped tears. Some consoled her mother. Her father placed his hand on Aasiya's head and uttered a blessing. Her brother watched over her protectively as she walked towards the rented car that would take her to her new home.

Aasiya turned her head back on her old life, walking away from it. The water looked further and further away.

The car started up.

The flowers on the graves withered, and the river went silent.

***

"Amma! Amma! Tell him to stop pulling my hair!" Aimal shrieked, swatting at her little brother.

Aasiya sighed. She pulled her youngest son away from her daughter before resuming her task. One last stitch added to her cloth before she held it up to see the outcome. *It would have to do.* The mistress of the tiny house they lived in paid Aasiya a small sum to stitch her clothes. It wasn't much, but life situations called for the extra money.

A yell from the children alerted her Abdul was back from work. She heaved herself off the floor and walked towards the door. On her way, she passed the window, glancing at the haggard figure looking back at her. She continued forward with a grimace.

"What's for lunch?" Abdul asked, throwing himself onto the rickety charpoy.

"Lentils with bread. We're out of flour, so there's just enough dough to make one *roti* for you." Aasiya rolled her eyes and waited for a reaction.

"Just one?! What the hell am I supposed to do with one *roti*, woman? I slave all day just to come home and starve?"

"Maybe if you didn't keep quitting jobs and earned enough money, we wouldn't be in this situation!" The same old argument again.

It was times like these when Aasiya missed being a child. She thought an adult's life was going to be fun and interesting. Stupidity really runs rampant in children. She used to dream of princes, lush green fields, riches beyond one's imagination, and a future as crystal clear as the river water once was. Instead, she was stuck with a lazy husband, screaming children, strained beyond her capabilities, and feeling dried out as the river water had become.

Such was life at 20.

Later the same day, she went to her brother's house. He had officially inherited it from their parents, who lived with him along with his wife. Aasiya went there when she needed to get out of the house, angry and frustrated with her husband. It happened a little too often.

Aasiya arrived, balancing little Fawad on her hip, while the other two children were managed with each hand. As she walked down the path, she thought of how lively the area used to be. Now there were just a few scattered huts and tents left. People had moved to the main village or city due to poverty. Most of them earned a living in agriculture, but farms were forced to shut down.

Children ran around, some barefoot. Babies wailed from hunger while mothers wearily shushed them. Elderly men stooped under the weight of bundles of branches carrying them from the dying forest to their homes. It was a miserable sight. Everything looked bleak.

Aasiya's children ran into the house. Aimal took Fawad and left Aasiya standing outside the doorstep. She looked out at the shallow trickle of water. Slowly, she made her way over to it. There was an overflow of graves several meters away from the water's edge. The earth on them, barren despite the onset of spring. It took a while to find the five original graves. Aasiya went and stood by them, uttering a quick prayer for each. She paused at the fifth. *Saima Bajwa. 11 years old.*

Cholera had reduced her sister's body to a frail nothingness. There hadn't been enough money to seek treatment. It still pained Aasiya to think of her little sister.

She sat on the ground, looking out over all the grave headstones. The land was drained of life. Where there had been greenery was now misery. The water that had once given the earth life was all gone.

She sat feeling as drained as the earth, aging earlier than she should, feeling the strain of her inner turmoil. The water choked and struggled as Aasiya tried to breathe. *What a sad sight to see.* A land without sustenance, a woman without life. Watch as it trickles away.

Watch. Away the water drains.

Radiyah Nouman

As a child, Radiyah Nouman witnessed Pakistani women living a common narrative. They traveled daily from distant villages as a desperate resort to support their families in distressed economic environments. Many were denied an education, married off at a young age, and subjected to the restrictive cultural norms for women. In her award-winning story, "Away the Water Drains," Nouman painted a poignant picture of what it is like to live through the eyes of a Pakistani girl in rural Southeast Asia.

Nouman won the grand prize for Kinsman Quarterly's Native Voice Award for Indigenous authors. Her story's protagonist, Aasiya, is "thrust into the complexities and harsh realities of village life and forced into an early adulthood." The young writer offered a parallel between the relentless life situation of the main character and the "untamable force of nature," a nearby river in gradual demise.

When asked about her inspiration for the story, Nouman said that it emerged from the cruel truth that "not everyone gets a happy ending." She felt it important to highlight "the resignation of millions of voiceless, faceless people who are hidden behind tales of heroes and happy endings."

"Pakistan and colonization have a long and bloody history," Nouman explained. "Our country people have had to lay down their lives just to be able to call our land our own. For decades, the subcontinent was under the rule of British colonizers who believed themselves to be our 'saviors.' Our people were servants on their own soil, soldiers to a government that wasn't their own, and pawns for a people who played chess with lives."

"There are many stories born from the blood spilled," Nouman told. "My people have evolved, but the West still holds its influence."

Although Pakistan reels from the historical impact of colonization, Nouman expressed her appreciation and love for her country.

"Pakistan is a very interesting country that is unfortunately misrepresented in the media. It has its struggles, and the political situation is almost always in turmoil, but there is a lot more to its people than meets the eye," Nouman said.

Khyber Pakhtunkhwa, one of the four provinces to which Nouman belongs, is known for its hospitality of smiles and good food. It is also home to some of the world's highest mountain ranges. Punjab is known for its fertile lands. Sindh is known for its rich cultural heritage preserved in sites like Mohenjo-Daro and architecture found in the city of Hyderabad. And Balochistan is abundant in natural resources.

"Pakistan is a lot more than the West thinks it is," Nouman shared. Pakistan is quite diverse, a place where followers of Islam, Christianity, Hinduism, Sikhism, Zoroastrianism, and Bahaism enjoy peaceful co-existence.

Nouman herself was raised apart from many gender norms of her country. She and her brother grew up without "stereotypical roles assigned."

"My parents never really ran on the 'men do this' and 'women do that' train of thought," the author told us. "It wasn't until I started going to an all-girls school from sixth to eleventh grade that I really became aware of the stark difference in treatment between men and women."

Nouman's mother is "a strong-willed and unshakable woman," traits the Pakistani author has grown to admire. "She taught me to never shy away, be confident in my thinking, and be bold with my words. My father is level-headed and observant, the one who encouraged me since childhood to grow to be an independent woman. These two helped me understand myself, the world around me, and made me want to help others do the same."

Unlike the girl in her story, Nouman has been given the exceptional opportunity to explore her interests in reading and writing. Both pastimes began as a hobby, but Nouman would soon recognize the transformative power of the two.

"I started finding myself wanting to express my frustration with the unfair treatment of different communities, women, and my country people. I hope to continue to use writing to advocate for such individuals and to encourage others to do the same."

When asked about the overall message she hoped to convey to the world through her writing, her answer was simple.

"If we want to see change, we need to bring about change. It is time to grow out of sympathy and acknowledgment; now is a time of action. If only all the Aasiyas are taught their worth and learn to live a worthy life and not let it waste away—to fight to revive life instead of watching it trickle away."

Radiyah Nouman

"Fake Ukhti"
Rizka Nafiah

*"That protest about my voice volume brought back memories
of my father's wish several years ago that I should be a calm
woman through a piece of veil."*
—Kalis Mardiasih, *Muslimah yang Diperdebatkan*

R eading the above excerpt from Kalis Mardiasih's book made
me realize that I am not the only one haunted by expectations
about my identity as a hijab-wearing Muslim woman. The difference
with me is that I didn't carry that burden of expectation from my
family.

I live in a semi-religious home. My parents are not strict adherents
of Islam but still require their children to fulfill the obligations to
worship and obey religious orders, including wearing hijab outside
the house. My family has never forced me to wear a long veil or a
long skirt, but it was the school rules that required me to wear hijab
to a certain standard.

No, I did not go to an Islamic school. Since elementary years, I attended a private school and mingled with non-Muslim students. However, my junior high school's principal at that time was quite religious. Girls were obligated to wear long skirts and veils that covered the chest, both for school uniforms and Muslim clothing during Islamic events. We were not allowed to wear trousers except during sports subjects. Eventually, this clothing style was carried over into my college life because I already felt comfortable with it.

I didn't consider how my hijab style might affect my self-representation. Not until I studied at a state Islamic university and started to get nicknames such as *ukhti* and *ustadzah*, Arabic words meaning *sister* and *teacher*. The words have literal meanings in their origin country, but in Indonesia the nicknames are also given to people who appear to be religious. At first, I ignored the jokes and kept expressing my interests by joining a debate community, discussing women's issues on social media, and being an anime fangirl. But then, a new nickname began to be attached to me: *ukhti yandere. Yandere* in Japanese means someone who looks sweet on the outside but is destructively psychotic on the inside.

When I started an internship at a company as a fresh graduate, I still got called *ukhti* by some coworkers. But once they found out I supported feminism, enjoyed skateboarding, and liked to shitpost and share memes, the nickname changed into *ukhti abal-abal* or "fake *ukhti.*" As if my identity as a human is only defined by my clothes, my identity as a Muslimah is disregarded, and my piety is considered untrue.

What the author Kalis and I experienced did not happen by chance. Human experiences have always been mediated by discourse. Thus, I can say that this experience is inseparable from the popular discourse about Muslim women, especially those who wear long hijabs, skirts, and socks. I remember two religious movies that were shown in cinemas and became so popular in Indonesia: *Ayat-Ayat Cinta (2008)* and *Ketika Cinta Bertasbih (2009)*. Both films feature romantic stories of a religious protagonist in Egypt. The common thread in these two films is the story of a humble man who is studying at Al-Azhar and meets the love of his life, a beautiful and pious woman wearing a long hijab—even *niqab* (a face covering). They get married and live happily.

The discourse in both movies portrays the main characters as ideal Muslim women with Ana wearing a long dress and long hijab covering her chest and Aisha sporting a long dress and *niqab*. Ana's character in *Ketika Cinta Bertasbih* is kind, graceful, and smart. In one of the iconic scenes, Ana is soothing her friend by hugging and rubbing her head gently. Meanwhile, Aisha in *Ayat-Ayat Cinta* wears more modest clothing and has a polite and religious character. When she meets Fahri, Aisha seems to lower her gaze because women are ordered to do so according to the religious discourse in Islam, particularly the Surah Qur'an An-Nur Verse 31 which states, "And tell the believing women to lower their gaze and guard their chastity, and not to reveal their adornments, except what (normally) appears."

When I watched those movies in junior high school, I witnessed how femininity and identity as a Muslim woman were shaped by society through clothing. I had no problem being myself before, yet I started to doubt my own identity as a Muslimah and wondered if I needed to change either my appearance or my hobbies. There were times when I felt like I didn't deserve wearing a long hijab and skirt, and other times I felt I was unable to express myself freely in public. So, over time I negotiated the way I dressed myself by starting to wear loose trousers instead of long skirts, and different styles of hijab that were still long enough to cover my chest. I did this to avoid looking too rigid or restricted as a Muslim woman and to express myself more freely in public, although I was perfectly fine wearing a long skirt.

The conversations about the ideal Muslim woman caused me to doubt my identity as a Muslimah and prevented me from expressing

17

myself freely. They rely on a regime that compels women to be less prominent in all their actions, categorizes human characters based on their looks, and restricts movement, thus narrowing the role of women in public spaces. In fact, anyone can have a tender personality, either men or women, regardless of their clothing style.

Over time, I have learned to be indifferent to the labels given to me. My identity as a Muslim woman will not crumble because I am an anime fan, like to share memes, or go skateboarding. Likewise, hijabs like Ana's and Aisha's can be worn by anyone regardless of their religion. Clothing is just one of the visible identities of a person, and that one identity by no means defines their entire life. After all, human identities are formed in an unstable and unfinalized social complexity.

Rizka Nafiah

Rizka Nafiah is an Indonesian linguist and a master's student of Media and Cultural Studies at Gadjah Mada University. Her essay "Fake Ukhti: The Issue of Hijab and the Abjected Identity of Muslim Women" placed as a finalist in the Native Voices Award.

In her poignant essay, she confronts the unreasonable schemas placed on women in her society and simultaneously roots herself within her own self-identity.

Nafiah recalled how she was often referred to as a "fake ukhti," a nickname given to her when she had her first job as a graduate.

"People called me that because I wore a long hijab yet supported feminism openly."

Those individuals, as Nafiah explained, failed to accept her strict Muslim attire along with her love of Japanese anime and enjoyment of reposting memes online.

"It is common to see women wearing hijab with various styles. However, there is an unspoken standard of piety that deems certain styles of hijab better than others."

According to Nafiah, approximately 86% of Indonesian people are Muslims, yet Islam has several streams. Indonesia consists of regions with 718 languages, each having different cultures and traditions. But like most places in the world, a woman is still judged by her appearance.

Nafiah, however, addressed the nonsensical aspects of expectations placed on Muslim women with her own defiance to remain unmoved by those expectations.

"I want to tell people that my identity as a human is not merely defined by clothes, and my identity as a Muslim woman won't be crumbled just because I did not fulfill the standard of piety made by society."

Battle of Broom:
Sweeping Mindsets
Vernica Goel

The foul smell of the drain is like rose petals; the dumping site with nothing but garbage piled is a sight for sore eyes; the sound of sweeping is music to my ears; the sharp thorns in the grass used to cover my body are as smooth as silk; the air filled with dust and dirt is fresh; because sweeping and cleaning is my purpose, my destiny, my life.
—Broom (Jhadu)

The birth of a broom takes place in the narrow lanes of the rural areas in Rajasthan and the by-lanes of Jodhpur city. The life of a broom will evoke a new emotion at every step. Sadness will hit you when you discover the reality of the caste system prevalent amongst broom-makers, garbage collectors, and municipal sweepers of India. Rage will surround you when you know about the age-old tale of the gender, socio-economic, political, and cultural division in these industries. Curiosity will arise when you read about the stories of countless superstitions associated with the most humble and inconspicuous object of everyday life.

The struggles and resilience of the people who make brooms are very real. They work without a roof over their heads. They clean houses, offices, and roads without access to clean drinking water. They are called "untouchables." Yet they do it every day because it is their livelihood. It is how they provide food for their families of ten or more. But this is not a livelihood they chose. This is a vicious circle of poverty they were born into and are forced to stay in. India became independent in 1947, but these Indian citizens, the most downtrodden caste groups, have never tasted that freedom.

The most disappointing part is what they experience daily— political apathy, untouchability, meager earnings, harassment, and humiliation by the hands of other Indian citizens who are supposed to be their brothers and sisters, per the National Pledge. The so-called upper and middle-class people are either blinded by their privilege or hiding behind the infamous line, "Yeh to kaafi saalo se hota aa raha hai," *This has been happening for so many years* that they forget the fact they are all humans at the end of the day. In communities like Jain, Aggarwal, Brahmin, Harijan, Akhateej Bhils, Bagaria, Bhatadia, and others, it is constitutionally unlawful to mistreat or discriminate against the untouchables, but the social norm is still prevalent in our society.

When people can't justify their actions and behaviour on moral grounds, they hide behind a thick veil of prevalent superstition as if sanctified by their holy books, the authenticity of which is impossible to prove.

They have their reasons to believe in superstitions, however logical or illogical. Sweeping early morning to erase the footsteps of the devils that were out at night; not sweeping after sunset as it is supper time for God Bavasi and the dust might go onto His plate; neither sweeping for at least 24 hours after the wedding of a daughter because you don't want to erase her footsteps; nor giving her a broom as a gift as it brings Lakshmi (*money*) and you don't wish to give it away; not stepping over a broom; not hitting it; keeping it at a height or in a sleeping position hidden inside the house; not hitting a child with a broom as in next life, you will be a slave to that child for as many years as there were twigs in the broom; not buying a broom on Tuesdays and Saturdays as those are inauspicious days, but buying a broom on Dhanteras as that is an auspicious day; offering a broom to Jharu Baba so that he fulfills your wishes. These are harmless superstitions that people believe because they want to. Our job is not to judge them for these superstitions but to respect their beliefs.

A broom made of peacock feathers is used for dusting the pictures of gods in a shrine and for curing illness with a tap on the head using tantra-mantra. A broom made of Vipuno, Buado, Heenyo, and Kheemp is for sweeping outside the house, while a broom made of Khejur, Alya, or Daab is for sweeping inside. Phool Jharu is used to clean concrete floors. All these are not only based on the different materiality and cost of the broom, but also the traditional knowledge and the superstitions associated with it.

It is said that a woman is uncultured if she scatters the broomsticks while sweeping. It is better to clean with a bent hand than a straight hand. If a daughter-in-law doesn't sweep properly, she is sent back to her parents' house, and a new wife is picked for the household. The men of the household do not even touch a broom, as sweeping the house is considered a woman's job. It is hard work with no pay. On the other hand, making and selling a broom is hard work with low margins, and those margins are getting narrower as human labour is being replaced by machines. Their livelihood is being threatened.

The broom is considered an auspicious object and is worshipped in our country. Yet the people who make it and use it are considered untouchables. The people who clean our houses, offices, roads, schools, colleges, institutes, and our spaces are considered dirty and impure. The irony is not lost.

To say that broom-makers lead a difficult life would be a massive understatement. Unfortunately, they can't turn the broom into a magic wand and fly away from poverty. Thus, each day they wake up and treat those brooms like swords to fight and live another day. Their battle with the broom would be a lot easier if we could sweep the caste system and the cobwebs of untouchability out of our mindsets.

Vernica Goel

Vernica Goel is a multifaceted artist: a trained Kathak dancer, a professional watercolor artist, product designer, and an aspiring entrepreneur. Her interests include reading non-fiction, playing lawn tennis, and creative writing.

Through her writing, Goel aspires to raise awareness about social issues, particularly those related to caste-based discrimination and the challenges faced by marginalized communities. She delves deep into cultural explorations, showcasing the diversity and nuances of different societal practices that evoke understanding and empathy.

"I pride myself on my empathy, inclusivity, and cultural sensitivity," Goel told Kinsman Quarterly. "I was born in India, a developing country, and I want nothing more than to live in India, a developed country. But that development should not come at the risk of modernization and encroachment on our ancestral lands, tribal cultures, and the resilience of marginalized groups."

Goel described her country as having a rich cultural heritage, diverse traditions, and a history spanning thousands of years.

"It is home to several major religions, including Hinduism, Islam, Christianity, Sikhism, Buddhism, and Jainism. Each religion has its own set of beliefs, rituals, and festivals, contributing to the mosaic of diversity and a unique tapestry of traditions. Indian society places a strong emphasis on family and community. The social structure historically includes the caste system."

India's caste system is a hierarchical social structure traditionally dividing Hindus into four main categories (varnas): Brahmins (priests), Kshatriyas (warriors), Vaishyas (traders), and Shudras (laborers). Below these are the Dalits (formerly known as "untouchables"). The system dictates social status, occupation, and marital possibilities, historically enforcing strict segregation and discrimination. Though officially abolished, its social implications persist in modern India. Currently, there are considerable efforts to address and overcome its negative aspects on the Indian population.

Goel's essay, "Battle of Broom: Sweeping Mindsets," was placed among the finalists of the Native Voices Award. It is a portrait of the struggles and challenges faced by India's Dalit community. The piece captures the community's plight and advocates for breaking down the ingrained prejudices, marginalization, and caste-based discrimination embedded in societal mindsets. Inspired by the documentary "Jharu Katha: Broom Stories" by Navroze Contractor, Goel explores the lives of individuals engaged in occupations related to broom-making, garbage collection, and municipal sweeping.

The author's message is a call to action, urging all to reflect on their attitudes and biases and to work towards creating a more inclusive and just society. Goel wants others to "recognize the dignity and humanity of every individual, regardless of their caste or occupation."

Vanilla Life
Shrinidhi Darbhe

I came home on a Tuesday as usual. Every time I entered after dark, silence greeted me. Some days, the silence accompanied an emptiness so heavy it dimmed my confidence. But whenever I saw my wife's face, the troubles amounted to nothing. She wore a smile and love reserved only for me.

That Tuesday became the toughest of my life because she was gone. Everything that was her—her mugs, her coffee, her scent, her smile, her love—all replaced by her absence.

It's not like I didn't see it coming. For the past year, she slowly withdrew from the life we built.

We'd have dinner together every day, and over dinner, she'd tell me how Keiko, her best friend, found her 100th love for the 100th time; a guy who was perfect.

"She met him while camping in Yamanashi. His eyes were beautiful and deep, she said." Then my wife turned to me. "How can you tell if someone's eyes are deep?"

"I can tell," I replied. My wife's eyes lit up. She loved to listen to solutions and answers. That was her thing—figuring out the answers to the world's questions. Perhaps she was trying to find an answer to her own questions.

"I wanna know how. Please tell me!" she said. And there it was—her child-like curiosity.

"Ok, I will," I said. "It's very simple. Look at my eyes; look very carefully. Are they deep?"

"I can't tell. That's the whole point. They just look like a pair of eyes to me."

"Now look at me. What do you feel?"

"Something—" she replied shyly.

"Something?"

"Well, you know. I feel mush."

"Well, there you go. That's your answer," I told her. "It's not the answer that needs revealing, but the question. When someone says 'your eyes are deep,' they're answering the question, 'what do I feel for you?' The answer is *love*. I see the world in your eyes because you are my world."

"So, you mean this is probably the 100th time she's seen deep eyes?"

"Yes."

And we laughed together, looking into each other's eyes.

That night, while in bed, I thought to myself, *why didn't she see depth in my eyes?* Why did I have to carry her to the answer? Maybe she was focusing too much on the technicalities to notice it was me she was looking at—the love of her life. Before I put the thought to sleep with me, I recalled a recent occasion.

We went grocery shopping and somehow, we again fell into a talk about Keiko. This time, Keiko was obsessed with a salaryman who loved golf and could smell the change of seasons. It was the season-smelling that apparently interested Keiko.

"It made him seem human, according to her," my wife said.

"What was he before that? An ogre?"

"Don't be mean."

"I am not. I'm just asking."

My wife went on about the golf boy as I loaded the cart, wondering if she ever talked about me with Keiko. If she ever said, "he can work his way around the kitchen" or "he is a nice listener" or "he can wash dishes."

Come to think of it, I had never given her many reasons to obsess over me. I now realize how boring I am.

That day in the store, my wife held up a cup of vanilla ice cream from down the aisle. And shamelessly, I nodded yes. Yes to being absolutely vanilla.

Shrinidhi Darbhe

Shrinidhi Darbhe, author of "Vanilla Life," is a literature fanatic with an avid interest in daytime dreaming. Nocturnal by nature, she enjoys writing in the dead of the night. Her work is often centered around the mysterious, tinged with themes of cultural peculiarity.

The Indian author explained that she is from a religious and spiritual people but doesn't personally subscribe to many of the popular beliefs. She does, however, "realize the mental backbone that such positivity provides."

Darbhe suggested that there is an unwavering influence of art in her culture that "is stunning and at times transcendental."

"We tell mythical stories through traditional dance forms of 'Bharatnatyam' which might not look very exciting, but it leaves a lasting impression. Once you dive into this world of spiritual artistry, it's hard to come back. And I personally enjoy being stuck in this mystical maze of complex culture."

According to Darbhe, her flash fiction piece is an exploration of a singular idea: How would it feel to nurture an escapist world in your head, and what would you do if, at the peak of your obsession, you couldn't escape with it?

"I mean, that sounds like a lot more than just one idea, but it's tough to pinpoint where the actual idea lies," Darbhe said. "Now that I think about it, it might be more of an exploration of a feeling than a solid idea."

When asked about the message of her story, Darbhe said, "I did not intend for there to be a message but for there to be an aftertaste. I wanted to engage the audience in fiction and then leave them on a cliffhanger, which in this case became an open-ended interpretation of the story."

Darbhe further told Kinsman Quarterly that she drew inspiration for "Vanilla Life" during her time in Japan.

"It's a place that evokes a feeling that's very indiscernible. It outweighs you and you feel the effects long after you've left. I wanted to convey those [effects] for sure."

"As a writer... I've always been impressed with prose that can pull you in," Darbhe admitted. The writer prefers to leave it up to the reader to make final sense of a piece. "Kinda like Einstein scrambling in his later years to find a theory of everything. I put those two motivations together to see what I could come up with."

Shrinidhi Darbhe

The Americas

Section

2

Cause and Effect
Alysha Brooks

The Lost Ones

No one was left alive.

When they left, *if* they left,

they left everything behind,

but

the trauma

the pain

the torture

that was laced inside their veins.

Alysha Brooks

They were only children

when they went in.

Left as corpses, broken souls.

This is Genocide;

no funerals for the ones that did not survive.

Instead, a pit filled with tiny corpses—

killed,

for daring to breathe the white man's air.

Not so ancient Indian burial grounds—

1996, just 22 years ago

—was when the last slaughterhouse closed.

Kill the Indian, save the man.

Translation:

Kill the Indian, save the white man.

But you can't have a white man of red skin.

Assimilation is a myth.

Translation:

kill the Indian,

kill the Indian,

kill the Indian.

Break the Indian,
rape the Indian.
throw the Indian

out the window.

It doesn't matter;
he is not human,
he is a savage.

Kill the Indian,
kill the Indian,

kill the Indian.

Alysha Brooks

The Sorry Girl

Sorry for my love.

Sorry for my hate.

Sorry for walking too fast too slow.

Sorry for talking or not talking at all.

I'm sorry,

I'm sorry,

I'm so sorry,

I'm so so sorry,

I'm sorry I'm sorry...

I'm sorry

I exist.

I'm sorry for taking up too much space.

I'm sorry you have to look at me.

I'm sorry for you and I'm sorry for me.

I'm sorry for breathing your precious air.

I'm sorry you branded your screams

in my head like maggots.

I'm sorry, I can't stop saying sorry,

because I think that's the only way

to make you stop

because I've must've done something wrong.

Yes, I must've done something wrong.

That's why you scream until my ears bleed.

Tell me I'm a creature, a monster,

something evil, anything.

So tell me why I'm sorry

because I don't know.

And I don't think *you* know...

do you?

Are you?

Sorry?

Alysha Brooks

The Life of a Tree That Mars the Grave

Is this the forgetting
or is this a new? Life
from death, the cracking
of the casket, the breaking
of the tomb.

Life born of death;
death born of life.

Is the way
is the new day, is the dawn
is this it... is it goodbye?
Sweetly, to heaven; sweetly,

to rest. Beauty from beauty
Stolen from the dead. The pit
from the body, from the seeds
sprout the roots.

Bring her up to me,

bring her up to me,

bring her

a new life.

Living from the dead,

creation from the person

I once knew.

This tree

This life

is it truly the new you

or is this the world simply forgetting,

simply forgetting you?

Alysha Brooks

How to Live on Stolen Time

I fear

    the future

I fear

    my life

ticking

closer

to something

to anything

to everything

and nothing.

For what am I?

But one who lives on stolen time.

One whose life itself is stolen,

or at least it should've been,

According to them,

of course.

It always is

according to them.

The thieves of our past:

an unfortunate present,

a rule book written by criminals,

a legal theft.

I think of them:

the stolen ones,

their stolen ways,

the waste of all the things they take.

Not knowing the weight

of not knowing

their ways.

We are waste,

to them.

But I cannot let them go to waste.

I think of them:

the ones who never returned,

the ones below

the stolen earth.

We walk with the dead,

Alysha Brooks

Holding those never forgotten.

For they live inside us,

our heart

beating

pumping

thumping

our shared blood.

We are the ghost they could not kill.

Inside of us,

they live.

With each stolen breath,

I give them my life.

We are one,

a reincarnation of our power.

We won the game

of life and death.

A people reborn with each generation.

You cannot take our soul.

Inside us

we heal the wounds of old.

We comfort the dead.

We will make you remember!

You cannot erase those you cannot kill.

We live to take back what is rightfully ours.

Our lives, our ways, our truth

are not yours to take,

to shape.

Our future

is ours

and yours too

is in our hands.

The power of them

to make the change

is what makes me afraid,

sometimes.

Alysha Brooks

To do something
to do anything
to everything

and nothing.

But is this enough to make them proud?
For what change is worth their death
or life
simply stolen away.
But now there's nothing to do
but to be free
to have joy
to be proud of who we are
to live without shame
to hold our children close
to do all that was stolen away from them
to live a life worth living
for all of us.

With every stolen breath
with every step
we make them proud.

Alysha Brooks

Alysha Brooks, author of the "Cause and Effect" poetry collection, never imagined she would be a writer. Having severe dyslexia, Brooks has had to approach her love of literature through reading and writing software. Her first short story, "Dyslexia," is being published with *Dreamers Writing Collective*. "Cause and Effect" in the *Native Voices* anthology marks her second publication.

"I was constantly told that I was an idiot because I could not read or write, and now I am writing winning pieces for magazines. Like many native and oppressed people, I have never had the privilege to dream. So now that I have begun [dreaming], I do not want to limit myself."

The writer now lives in Canada but doesn't identify as a Canadian. She is a member of the Lax Kw'alaams Band, but her mother's Dutch side grants her the advantages of passing as White. Brooks briefly describes living within that dichotomy.

"I am mixed with both oppressed and oppressor. I often know that my skin is threatening to my people, as theirs is threatening to the colonizers. In native spaces, I get looks. They wonder if I am another invader. In White spaces, I am the native they take seriously. I am threatening because I don't look like the threat. That's why I think using my privilege is so important."

Brooks explained that she is in a special position to live between two worlds and finds it unfortunate that due to colonization, it is on the side of the native people to force the colonizers to understand their own history.

Brooks was born into a family of activists. Her grandfather lost most of his Tsimshian culture in residential schools but passed what he could in "reduced form." According to Brooks, traditional native culture is tied to specific people with specific lands and territories. Their traditions have been passed down through clans and generations, but because of colonization, many natives have limited access to their traditional culture; therefore, urban native culture was born.

"The root of the culture is our trauma. We come together at beading fairs, Indigenous school initiatives, and youth groups. We share our stories of oppression from the Indian Act, the 60s Scoop, and, of course, residential schools. We bring together what little teachings we know, creating a patchwork garment that doesn't quite fit, but is close enough."

"My collection of poems speaks to this urbanized native culture, not only focusing on our collective trauma, but also personal accumulation of intergenerational trauma."

When asked about the message of her poetry collection, Brooks said, "I would say that the overall message revolves around provoking that same sort of patchwork feeling that resides in urbanized native spaces."

Within those native spaces, Brooks explained that there are big topic issues, including murdered Indigenous women, the 60s Scoop, the millennial Scoop, and residential schools, but there is also the "lingering of less certain connections."

"The vague feelings of things just slightly being off—anxiety, depression, strange ailments among our people, and general mistrust," Brooks explained. "A lot of our dysfunction stems from intergenerational trauma. Because it is not necessarily our trauma to hold, we don't know what to do with it. It's just there in the pits of our stomachs."

Brooks went on to share how her grandfather is the source of her inspiration for the collection.

"He unknowingly created the foundations for what I believe is urbanized native culture," Brooks explained, "He, alongside my grandmother, taught me how the government took most of what we were away. They could kill us, they could lock us in prisons, torture us, they could take our lands and our children, but what they could never take was our spirit."

Alysha Brooks

Trauma is My Birthright
Brooke Waukau

October 27, 2016

It was a cold fall morning at Treaty Camp on the Standing Rock Sioux Reservation, where North Dakota law enforcement and Energy Transfer Partners violated Article II of the Fort Laramie Treaty and carried out countless human rights violations.

"Wake up! Hey, wake up! They're coming down the road!"

I rubbed my eyes as my heart pounded faster. My body couldn't rouse as fast as the panic set in. Disoriented, I pulled back the canvas of the teepee; sunlight pierced my eyes. Fire had been burning for a week straight. An anxious anticipation shone in the eyes of the people scrambling around our makeshift camp. I walked up the ditch and onto the road but couldn't see anything.

I approached the first person I saw. "I don't see them! He said they were coming down the road."

A man handed me his binoculars and calmly replied, "Here look—about half a mile up there. They're just moving very slow."

They queued up in such unison they appeared as one black horizontal line. My hands and arms went numb at the sight of them. I knew what was coming next.

"Thanks," I said with a lump in my throat before continuing back towards camp.

I heard another man yell *"Light 'em up!"* He pointed to a pile of tires strategically set for the main camp down the road, a signal that Morton County PD was coming.

Four men jumped into the back of a rusty pickup truck. The exhaust roared, and the men let out war cries. The sheer pitch and visceral sound sent chills up my spine. I couldn't help thinking about my ancestors feeling the same way since 1492.

My brain rejected the notion of fighting the same battles centuries later. I grabbed a Red Bull out of my bag and chugged it, hoping to wake my sleep-deprived body. It was survival time, and my body never missed an opportunity to be traumatized for the right reasons.

Remaining at the camp all week, we had been able to hold off construction. We cost Energy Transfer Partners millions in losses, a little light at the end of our tunnel. Deep down, I knew the momentum would end.

Black smoke filled the sky, and our people piled anything they could find to make a barricade in the road. An old car, wooden pallets, tires, and broken fencing—all creating a false sense of security.

With every week that passed, with every interaction with Morton County, the violence escalated. They wouldn't disappoint their shareholders any longer. We knew they were coming at us with everything they had.

The rhythmic thuds in the sky from the helicopter got closer. They needed to do some recon before approaching. I imagined them asking, *What do the Indians have in store for us today?* Their original plan was for the Dakota Access Pipeline to go through Bismarck, but the enemies of the sun and their communities did not want an oil pipeline contaminating their soil and water. *Go figure.* So, they ran it under Lake Oahu, the only clean water source for the Standing Rock Sioux Tribe, along with countless others. No consultation, no environmental impact statement, no regard for human or animal life, and no regard for the land and the water. The path of least resistance. Well, so they thought.

I heard someone in the distance yell, *"We're starting a prayer circle on the direct path of construction. Whoever sits in this circle is getting arrested today!"*

Without hesitation, I knew that was where I needed to be. I ran back to the teepee to grab my goggles, mask, and earplugs. The ear plugs were new to my frontline gear, but necessary to block out the long-range acoustic device sound cannons. I threw on my goggles to prevent the pepper spray from penetrating my eyes and the mask to mitigate the amount I would inhale.

I looked around the teepee and sat down. It was so calm. I took it in for a moment, knowing the chaos that would shortly unfold. Immense gratitude emerged in that moment. For the last few nights, I had the privilege to occupy the teepee, experiencing things I never thought I would in my lifetime; watching the stars from its inside, sitting around the fire, sharing stories and lots of laughter with indigenous relatives from all over the country. There was beauty within this horror.

Sleep deprivation could not affect the adrenaline coursing through my body. Many elders joined us on the ground. There was so much courage and uncertainty in that circle. My emotion of choice was usually anger. Anger fueled me. That deep anger, that protective anger, the type of anger that changes you. Anger at the repeated attacks on my people, anger at the lack of humanity, anger at the police who enjoyed the brutality they inflicted upon us. No one was exempt from that brutality: women, children, and even elders. This was physical, psychological, and spiritual warfare.

Brooke Waukau

Brooke Waukau is the third-place winner of the Native Voices Award and a member of the Stockbridge Munsee Band of Mohicans and Menominee Nation. Waukau is a graduate student at the University of Wisconsin-Oshkosh and has a BA in Public Administration from the College of Menominee Nation. She is the founder of Women's Indigenous Media, a nonprofit media organization founded in Standing Rock, North Dakota.

Her award-winning essay, "Trauma is my Birthright," is a snapshot of modern-day genocide and navigates through the experience of the physical, psychological, and spiritual warfare that exists for Indigenous people in America and all over the world.

When asked about the message she hoped to convey to the world within her essay, Waukau broke it down.

"Climate change is here. The militarization of law enforcement is here. The trauma and abuses private corporations inflict through the theft and rape of our land, water, and people is here. Understanding how that trauma is passed down through generations and holding space for those emotions is the real strength behind our "resilience".

Waukau is the first documented female Native American drone pilot. She and other drone pilots' aerial footage allowed them to document the human rights and due process violations occurring on the Standing Rock Reservation. In 2021, Waukau began her role at the Department of Justice as the Missing and Murdered Indigenous Women's Task Force Coordinator.

Being an advocate for her community, Waukau talked about her inspiration for her social justice efforts and writing.

"My inspiration comes from my children, future grandchildren, and all the generations that come after me," Waukau said. "Accurately documenting my experiences is extremely important to me along with the obligation I feel to share it with the world."

When asked about her feelings on the colonization that has impacted her people, Waukau said, "The continued theft of Indigenous-occupied land has and will continue to destroy the world. Extractive colonialism has committed countless crimes against Indigenous people, from climate change to our missing and murdered Indigenous women and children."

"My writing aspirations are to write a book telling my whole truth so that future generations will learn from the past and take those lessons into the future."

Indian Ice
Dr. Deidra Suwanee Dees

You taught me

i was

    not

    born

biologically

    savage

until

you   taught

    me

i was

Dr. Deidra Suwanee Dees

Indian Sin

sunday

    school

        teacher taught
        us Indians

we

    were

        born into
        original sin,

and jesus

    paid

        for our
        sin.

teacher,

    if jesus

        paid for our
        sin,

why

    do
        I
        have to pay?

Dr. Deidra Suwanee Dees

Not For Sale

andrew jackson called my name
to see if he could dispute his blame
for killing off the redstick men
at the battle of horseshoe bend.

mr. jackson, it's too late
for you to renegotiate,
mvskoke land was not for sale,
now you will always burn in hell.

white slaver called my name
to see if he could oppose his blame
for killing off african people
under protection of the steeple.

mr. slaver, it's too late
for you to try to repudiate,
human beings were not for sale,
you must accept your place in hell

Buy and Sell

your grandmothers

     were owned by white people
—my people were not

they did not buy and sell us,
they did not force us to cook for them

     —clean toilets
     pick cotton

they did not
     force us to lay down for them

but now—we do it for free

Damaged

polluted   culture

damaged by   invasion

        in all my years

growing up on   dog river

no one

ever taught   me

where
        the   sun rises

Mvskoke Boy
Dr. Deidra Suwanee Dees

<u>First Grade</u>

When school ended at the one-room schoolhouse, I grabbed Birdie's hand, and we headed for home. We ran and we ran, trying to get past the white boys, 'cause they laugh at us and beat us up when they can catch us. The white boys say we're no good 'cause we're Mvskoke Indians.

Robert Davis said he was gonna take me behind the schoolhouse tomorrow and scalp me. I told the teacher when Billy Ray said the same thing last week, but she's white, too. So, she didn't do nothing about it, of course.

As we ran past John Gulsby's house, he yelled for everybody to hear, "Otis Dees is a poor Indian Redskin!"

"Try to keep up with me," I told Birdie. And ran faster than I thought I could.

When we got home, me and Birdie got a drink of ice-cold water from the giant dipper in the well. Then, we fed the chickens and the cow. Mama told me to ring a chicken for supper, but *Birdiehadtocookit; Birdiehadtocookit.*

Mama couldn't cook 'cause she was too sickly to get out of bed. I think she might be gonna to have a baby or some kind of grown-up stuff like that.

Second Grade

Last spring, the mule bucked the plow when Daddy was planting the cotton, so Daddy broke his hip. Now, I gotta do all the work on the farm. I just wish I could get paid for it. But I'm old enough to know that Indians ain't got no money.

"Otis, Otis! Come here, Otis!" Mama hollered.

I knew she had something for me to do from that calling. I climbed down from the dogwood where me and Birdie climbed to the top and ran into Mama's kitchen to see what she wanted.

"You take this sugar to Coosah, Otis, okay? You feed all this sugar to the horse—you hear me?"

"Yes, ma'am," I told her, intending to do what she said.

As I headed to the barn, my nose caught a scent of the molasses in my hand. *I bet that sugar tastes good!* Like the candy white children brought to school in their lunch pails. Like lollipops in the "Big Store" that Indians couldn't afford. Shoot. Since the stock market crash, even some of the whites can't afford 'em.

When I was out of Mama's eyeshot, I pushed my face right into the pile of sugar and took the biggest bite I could. Rocky, gritty, then melting like syrup, sliding down my throat. Sugar rush.

I shoved my hand under Coosa's mouth. "Here's your sugar, ole boy," I told him. "Pretty boy, gentle boy."

I rubbed Coosah's face as he nibbled and slobbered. He looked up and nudged the side of my head, wetting my hair as though asking, *where's the rest of my sugar?*

I halfway ducked, caught myself. I really shouldn't be bothered by Coosah's slobber. After all, it was a small price to pay for stealing his sugar.

Daddy looked more sickly than I ever saw him. He said Mama had two babies last night. Ms. Della, the negro wife, tried to help, but both babies died. Daddy said it was strange that while he slept in front of the fireplace, a *haint* like a fireball woke him up, shot from between his toes, and went up the chimney. That was the same time the babies died.

Third Grade

Joey Cramer went to school with me, and his mama said she was tired of all that politicking going on down there at the white church. She came over last Sunday and picked me up by the arm and slung me up in the back of the wagon with Joey. Off we went to the whiteman's church. Some of the men made me sit on the floor 'cause they said Indians ain't allowed to sit on the benches with whites. That made Ms. Cramer as mad as a hornet. But we sat on the floor all the time at home.

The preacher told a story about a baby born in a faraway land. He said the baby was born to die so all people can go up to heaven... *even Indians.* He said whoever wanted to go up to heaven must go up to the front.

I ran up to the front of the church house. "Preacher man, Preacher man, I wanna ask baby Jesus to take me to heaven."

But it didn't do me no good. You see, Ms. Cramer caught that tuberculosis that was going around, and she died that winter. That ended that. I don't care nothing about going to the whiteman's church anyhow.

Fourth Grade

I wanted to learn some schooling but just can't catch up to the fifth graders. I wish I read as fast as them. My oldest sister Ruby said I should be thankful for getting to go to the whiteman's school. Sometimes I got tired of hearing her say it. The government didn't pass the law so Indians can go to school until Ruby was eleven. She must of caught up 'cause she's in ninth grade now.

My cousins Jesse and Wesley told us to come over to play last Saturday. I was glad they did 'cause I wouldn't have nobody to play football with. Me and Birdie went over to their house and played football all day long. On accident, I hit Jesse in the head with the football, and I knew his mama was gonna whup me when she saw his black eye.

Joey Cramer and some sixth graders let me play marbles with them this morning at school. The reason why—they wanted the marbles Jesse gave me. But I won their marbles! I don't expect they'll be asking me to play again.

Fifth Grade

Mama was still kindly sick, but she was going to visit Aunt Queenie in the big city down in Mobile. I helped her hook up Coosah to the wagon to go catch the train for her trip.

I earned twenty-five cents last week picking cotton for old man Gladshaw. I was saving it up to get a secondhand football. But mama asked if she could borrow it for her trip, so I gave it to her.

Jack Kindle, who lived behind us, said one of the boys down the road got an indoor outhouse. I didn't want one of those due to the bad smell. Ain't nothing wrong with our outhouse. Only thing was—it's a long ways to walk at night when it's cold, and I didn't like using the slop jar.

When I came in from school today, daddy told me mama died—in Atmore—coming back from Aunt Queenie's. The whiteman at the train station told daddy he wanted to take mama to the hospital, but Indians ain't allowed in the hospital. Mama died right there in the train car. I was glad I lent her my twenty-five cents. I didn't mind that I'd never get it back.

Right after daddy told me about mama, visitors came up in the front yard. Me and Birdie ran under the house to hide. We didn't know all the people that came over, but they said they was our relatives. I never seen so many Mvskoke Indians in all my life.

Daddy seen us hiding through the cracks in the floor and made us come out. He said we had to have a proper introduction to our relatives.

It didn't bother me before, but now it was hard for me to think about stealing Coosah's sugar. I think that was the only time—the only time—I ever disobeyed mama.

Sixth Grade

There's some negro boys that lived across Dees Creek behind us, where Ms. Della lived. They came across the creek today. I hid in the bushes, so as to get a good look at 'em. The teacher said, "Don't go near them 'cause, if they touch you, your skin will turn black as soot." I took a good look at them boys, and there weren't a one of 'em black. They were brownish color like me.

A whiteman rode his horse from the county seat to our house with saddle bags full of papers. He told us we gotta get new birth certificates on account of the fire that burned the courthouse down in September. He said the papers inside burnt clean up. But Daddy said birth papers ain't important to Indians. That's something the whiteman made up to find out how many of us there were.

Seventh Grade

Johnny Blacksher went to school with me. His mama cooked fried fish and said I could come over and eat dinner with them on Sunday. I wondered why 'cause they ain't Indians.

They had the best fish and supper—mashed potatoes, sliced tomatoes, fried okra. Kinda like mama used to make. Johnny's mama even gave us a CocaCola in a see-through glass bottle.

Since the stock market crashed, a lot of people couldn't buy things like that. We ain't ever afforded 'em. Daddy said they ain't no good for you no way.

Daddy asked if the fish was from the ocean in the Gulf of Mexico, the saltwater kind. I told him Johnny said his uncle caught the fish in the Alabama River near the bluff where Red Eagle and his horse jumped into the river to keep from being killed in the Red Stick War.

"You shouldn't *never* eat that saltwater fish," Daddy said. "I went to town and saw a peddler who had some saltwater fish on sale. It was all the fish you can eat for five cents, which woulda been a good deal, but it was too salty to eat."

Eighth Grade

It was almost dark when I came in from hunting. There were two horses hitched to two wagons in the front yard and an automobile. We ain't never had no automobile in our yard before. One of the wagons was like the covered wagons in the Wild, Wild West; the kind cowboys said Indians shot with arrows for no blame reason. Those folks were just ignorant. But cowboys stealing our land, taking our food, and treating us like poor Indian trash sounded like a good enough reason to shoot 'em all slap up.

When I went inside to see all that was going on, Ruby met me at the door and told me Daddy had died. He was sickly for a long time, just like Mama. Our relatives came to get him ready for the funeral and laid him on his and Mama's bed.

Birdie was in an awful way. I was fourteen now—supposed to be a man about it—but I had to get away from the house, go into the woods, and just *let loose*. I especially didn't wanna let Birdie see me crying. Indians ain't allowed to cry.

Ninth Grade

They built a new schoolhouse 'cause the old one burned down last summer. The new one's got lots of rooms and made of red bricks. It was even two stories high with upstairs classrooms.

Now that I was in ninth grade, the white boys didn't pick on me half as much as they used to. I grew bigger than all of 'em. They quit fighting me 'cause I began winning.

Tenth Grade

I was playing high school football for the Blacksher Bulldogs. We beat all the schools in the South. I got my first football letter at the end of last season. The white boys called me Square Dees 'cause they said I could knock a square hole in the line of defense.

Me and Birdie missed Daddy. I wish he coulda been around to see me play football with the skinny white boys, the ones that used to make fun of me for no reason—no reason at all except 'cause I was born a poor Mvskoke boy.

Dr. Deidra Suwanee Dees

Injustice

Dr. Deidra Suwanee Dees

"What's wrong? *What's wrong?*" I asked Mr. Otha Martin. The elder, who was fondly referred to by the community as Uncle Otha, shook his head and would not tell me.

I was working on collecting data on the Mvskoke Education Movement for my dissertation at Harvard. I had come to continue my interview series with him. He and his wife, Ms. Marie, welcomed me into their home, but an uneasiness sat in the air.

I broke out my handheld recorder to continue our interview on barriers to public education for Mvskokes in his generation, but Uncle Otha appeared distracted and anxious.

"What is wrong?" I asked, looking directly into his eyes.

"Come on. Come with me," he beckoned, walking out the back door. He insisted I get into his truck before he continued our interview session. I climbed in with recorder and notebook in hand. Lumbering around in his boxy farm truck on bumpy back roads, he drove to a desolate road where two roads diverged a few miles east of the Massachusetts Trail.

He parked his truck in the middle of the road and turned off the engine as though he would never start the truck again. Silence and daylight crowed my ears. No traffic around. Following his lead, I opened the truck door on my side as the summer drenched us in sweat.

"You've got to see this," Uncle Otha said, pointing to the side of the road.

He wanted me to witness the ecological injustice just below his fingertips. My eyes fell upon the *hopelkv ecohonvnwv*, deer graves, where 6 to 8 deer had been executed. No shame. Their bodies—exposed to approaching travelers—lay mangled, decaying in the sun, putrefying Mother Earth's bosom.

Uncle Otha lamented. "Can you believe this? Can you believe it? People treat the deer with no respect—no respect!"

The tenderloin meat had been butchered from the deer, exposing the hunters' wastefulness. They took only the coveted cut from their carcasses, leaving the rest to ruin.

He said whites took the best land from Mvskokes and built good houses and good schools for themselves. He described how they pushed the Indians upon the poorest quality of land, which prevented Mvskokes from having adequate land to grow food or to live on.

"The remaining land was so wet that a buzzard would get bogged down flying across it," he sniggered. Uncle Otha grew somber, shaking his head as water dripped earthward from his face. "Can you believe it? Who speaks for the deer? Who speaks for them? Why doesn't anybody speak for them?"

With the jerk of his arm, he pointed at me and said angrily, "I'm going to report this to the authorities."

Uncle Otha's protests paralleled a delegation of Native American leaders who expressed their concern for Mother Earth at the United Nations environmental conference. When given seats to sit in, the delegates asked, "Where is the seat for the deer? For the buffalo? For the eagle? Who speaks for them today?"

The delegation tried to educate world leaders on the ecological injustices that permeate Mother Earth, hoping to prevent further abuses. The leaders said that Native Americans are compelled to act as though "we are like a conscience; we are small, but we are not a minority; we are the landholders; we are the land keepers; we are not a minority, for our brothers are all the natural world, and for we are, by far, the majority."

As the deer lay decomposing in the blazing sun, the stench was almost more than I could bear. I thought about the analogy that Uncle Otha had drawn between the exploitation of the deer and the exploitation of Mvskokes. This stench, too, was almost more than I could bear.

Deidra Suwanee Dees

"Indigo—magenta," Dr. Dees wrote, moved at the sight of a sun-lit crest where her ancestors once admired the same landscape. She scratched words atop a Big Mac container. "Vanilla—tasting sky—" Capturing the beauty in real time, she embraced the poetic moment. She would not procrastinate to allow time to dull the image and the words taking shape in her mind.

Dr. Deidra Suwanee Dees, a member of the Mvskoke nation, sees poetry in every aspect of life. She often jots poems on make-do surfaces when a notepad isn't readily available. Her award-winning poem, "You Taught Me," is an example of the powerful free verse she pens in the moments of conception.

"You taught me" granted Dr. Dees the second-place win for Kinsman Quarterly's inaugural Native Voices Award. She summarized the poignancy of the poem: "Europeans taught us [Native Americans] that we were biologically savage. They taught us to hate ourselves. They taught us we needed to be colonized. After many years, we came to believe what they taught."

Dr. Dees explained that Westerners victimized Indigenous people with "colonization policies of the mind, body, and spirit."

"But once we figured them out," she said, "we began detoxification through decolonization writing such as this."

The journey of detoxification inspires Dr. Dees's work. She contributes to this process through her poetry and prose. In her upcoming publication, *Indian Ice: Indigenous Witness / Estv-Cate' Het'ute*, the Native American poet gathered a series of eyewitness poetry, which traverses a thirty-year span from 1994 to 2024. This collection is a witness to her transformative journey from suppressing her Mvskoke heritage to embracing her identity.

Dr. Dees grew up picking cotton on a rural Alabama farm, where her ancestors lived. Dr. Dees is a Cornell and Harvard graduate and the published author of *Vision Lines: Native American Decolonizing Literature*. Dr. Dees currently serves as Director / Tribal Archivist at the Poarch Band of Creek Indians and teaches Native American Studies at the University of South Alabama.

A Time For Dolls
Shantell Powell

SCENE 1

> A teenaged girl,
> PANIK, sings and plays
> with a doll while
> her mother, ANAANA,
> tends to a qulliq,
> an oil lamp used by
> traditional Inuit.

(A spotlight rests on
ANAANA who dresses the oil
lamp.)

ANAANA

(to audience)

A child is a blessing. Not every woman gets
with child, and not every baby survives ukiuq.
Her ataata made her the doll. He carved it

from the rib of a tuktu years ago, after she
survived her second ukiuq. Ukiuq is a hard
thing. It is the season when Sister Sun leaves
and Brother Moon returns twice to look for her.
Not every child lives so long. And every ukiuq,
others die, too. Children, brave ones, mothers,
elders. Some of all. Dolls are important.

> (As with the lighting of
> the qulliq, lights emerge
> onstage)

PANIK

I made the dresses myself.

> (The sound of a blizzard
> hisses in the background
> as the lights dim again.
> A GROUP of Inuit migrate
> across the stage.)

I softened the leather with my teeth and sewed
intestines without ripping them. Tell me a
story, anaana. Tell me about the hungry times.

ANAANA

This was before you were born. Blizzards buried
agluit and the seals didn't come. There were no
ptarmigan, char, or hares. No tuktuit. It was a
terrible time of starvation. It was past time
for us to migrate.

PANIK

Where did you go?

> (The GROUP of Inuit of all
> ages perform the physical
> action of ANAANA's story.)

78

We hear the sound of a
barking Arctic fox.)

ANAANA

We followed the distant barking of a fox, but
left behind those who were too weak to move. We
swore that when we found meat, we'd bring it
back. We promised, knowing that few, if any,
would survive. It was a tearful time, but if
the weak didn't stay behind, we'd all die.

PANIK

Who stayed behind?

(AUNTIE NAULAQ within the
GROUP shows distress with
a pregnant belly. A weary
GROUP freezes in place
when ANAANA pauses her
storytelling.)

ANAANA

The old. The sick. Your Auntie Naulaq with her
round belly. Her face gaunt as dried iqaluk.
All were starved and weak. (beat) Panik, you
are no longer a child. Your first blood has
come, and you must put away your doll. It is
time for your first tattoo.

PANIK

No, no, anaana. Not just yet, please. Tell me
what happened to the ones who were left behind.
To Naulaq.

(The onstage action resumes
with story. The weak and
elderly perform the giving,

79

chipping, and digging.
AUNTIE NAULAQ becomes alone
in her iglu, still holding
her pregnant belly.)

ANAANA

The oldest and the sickest were the first to
die. They gave what they had to Naulaq. A scrap
of dried iqaluk. A piece of hide. A worn-out
mukluk. But the blizzards worsened and they
were sealed up in their igluit, too weak to
chip away and dig themselves out. They died
tucked beneath hides which could no longer keep
them warm. They had little seal oil for the
qulliq. Naulaq was sealed up alone in her iglu,
too. She was alone save the little one kicking
her from the inside. I guess the baby kept her
warm enough to live.

PANIK

Did she have her baby?

(AUNTIE NAULAQ squats alone
to birth her baby, showing
intense pain and effort.)

ANAANA

It is hard to give birth. It is harder still
for one who is starving. How can you have the
energy to squat if you have not eaten? How
can you have the energy to hold your legs up
and open if you fall onto your back? How can
you push when you have used up your strength
chewing old mukluks? She let the qulliq go out.

(Lights go out, leaving
a spotlight on PANIK and

ANAANA. We see AUNTIE
NAULAQ vaguely in the
shadows.)

PANIK

Did she live?

ANAANA

The baby came out eventually, born into
darkness. She wouldn't light the lamp. She
pulled the baby to her nipple, but her breasts
were withered things full of dust instead of
milk. The smell of blood made her stomach groan
like a walrus. It had been too long since she'd
eaten. Far too long. The smell crazed her. In
the darkness, she lapped up the blood. Chewed
up the placenta.

PANIK

And then?

ANAANA

It kept her for a while. She was weak. She only
had a little seal oil left, and she refused to
light the qulliq. She didn't want to see. The
baby was weak and frail, and she had nothing to
feed it. She was still famished. And so, in the
darkness, she ate all that had come from her.

(Lights emerge. The GROUP
returns onstage with meat.
AUNTIE NAULAQ is in a fetal
position by the bones of
her baby.)

And when we came back with meat, it was too
late. When we came, we brought light, but she

81

would not open her eyes. We could not blame
her. The baby would not have lived. We saw
tiny, chewed-on bones.

                    PANIK

She ate her baby?

                    ANAANA

Yes.

                    PANIK

Oh.

                    ANAANA

She did not move again. She sat as though
paralyzed, frozen in one place, eyes always
closed. She lived for a time, when we fed her.
But...

          (The GROUP removes the
          limp body of AUNTIE NAULAQ
          offstage.)

... your time for dolls has passed, Panik.

                    PANIK

Tell me another story.

                    ANAANA

Of the bad times?

                    PANIK

Are there other times?

                    ANAANA

          (laughs)

PANIK

How am I to learn from the good times? Hard times are the best teachers.

ANAANA

An Inuk is someone who can make something from nothing. You will learn from everything, if you pay close enough attention. Like from your doll.

PANIK

Yes, like from my doll. I stitched the mukluks closed, doublechecked every stitch. Can't let the water and cold in. Must be warm and dry, even with such tiny mukluks. And I trimmed the ruff on the amauti with wolverine fur so it won't frost up.

ANAANA

You've done well. To sew such small things is important, but it is time to put them away.

PANIK

Not yet. Tell me more.

ANAANA

You should know to listen to your elders.

PANIK

I do, anaana. And to the angakoq.

ANAANA

Yes, the angakoq. Another story, then. There once was a man and a woman. They tried and tried, but couldn't make a baby.

83

(An exhausted MOON MAN
and WOMAN enter onstage.
They wearily go behind a
masking piece of the stage,
their action veiled to
the audience. Some faint,
laborious moans are heard.)

They had sex so much that they were sore and
chafed and panting like sled dogs. The woman
lay naked in the summer with her vulva exposed
to Moon Man, but her womb wouldn't quicken.
Moon Man impregnated all the other women, but
never her. It seemed that everyone had families
but her. Even some old grandmothers even had
a dozen children, but she had none. Moon Man
only paid enough attention to make her bleed a
little from time to time, but her belly never
bore life.

PANIK

Who was the Moon Man?

ANAANA

Moon Man is the Sun's brother. And the Sun was
the only woman with a vagina. Sun and Moon
were the only ones who had buttholes, but they
didn't know that, yet.

PANIK

You've got to be kidding! How did other people
shit?

ANAANA

They didn't. They didn't eat like us.

> (MOON MAN, WOMAN, and SUN
> WOMAN and the GROUP resume
> the physical actions of
> going into a camp, stocked
> well with meat.)

Anyway, Sun Woman and Moon Man decided they
wanted to take mates, so they went for a walk
and they found a hunting camp. Lumps of fat
and caribou were piled outside the igluit. The
people sucked on the meat and fat then spat it
out. There was no other way to get rid of it.

PANIK

How could there be people if there were no
vaginas?

ANAANA

Babies were cut from the womb with an ulu.
Then the mothers were sewn back up again with
caribou sinew.

PANIK

You're making this up!

ANAANA

No, it's true. So, Sun and Moon go to this camp
and make friends with everyone there.

> (CHARACTERS disappear
> behind the masking wall.
> Sounds of slicing and
> squealing can be heard.)

Sun Woman finds a man she likes, and before too
long, she gets pregnant. That was easy enough.
But when Moon Man finds a woman he likes, he was

in for a big surprise. She had no vulva! No vagina! But he wasn't worried. He took out his ulu, and carefully, he put it between her legs and made a slice.

PANIK

Ah! He cut her like maktaq?

ANAANA

(laughs)

Just so! She bled a little, of course. All mothers do. But the bleeding stopped, and she had a vulva and vagina.

> (Onstage actions resumes
> with WOMAN emerging from
> the masking piece, big and
> pregnant. Her water breaks,
> and she turns around
> quickly to return behind
> the masking wall.)

But Sun Woman was the first to give birth properly. Her water broke, and without needing a knife to help, a baby came out. Even better, it is the first baby to ever have a vagina and an anus. The people of the village were amazed, and decided they want these parts for themselves, too.

PANIK

I'll bet! What did they do?

> (We hear music, drums,
> slicing, and squealing.)

ANAANA

The women sang and danced with their frame
drums, and then they grabbed knives and sliced
their crotches open. Lo and behold, they all
got vaginas and vulvas.

(PANIK laughs.)

ANAANA

(recites as GROUP returns
onstage, each of them take
turns bending and jabbing
one another with forks)

Then everyone, men and women, grabbed forks and
stabbed themselves in the middle of their ass.
And that's how they got buttholes.

PANIK

That's what I call a party.

ANAANA

A wild one, for sure. They had a proper feast.

(GROUP switch their forks
into feasting motion,
gobbling as if it were food
to their mouths.)

Everyone could eat--really eat--and swallow
their food. And there was a lot of loving, too,
now that there was a much better way for babies
to come out of their mothers.

PANIK

There must have been a lot more people after
that.

ANAANA

Oh yes. The camps had to scatter across the
land, so there would be enough for everyone to
eat.

> (GROUP scatters offstage,
> except WOMAN AND MAN
> performing the actions of
> the story.)

PANIK

What happened to the man and the woman who
couldn't make a baby?

ANAANA

I was just getting to that. The woman laid on
the ground with her vulva exposed to the Moon,
but he ignored her. She was desperate. She
even got her husband to pretend to be a baby,
holding him in her arms and rocking him while
he suckled her breasts. But it was no good.
It wasn't the same at all. Finally, the woman
begged her husband to go find the angakoq. He
set off in his qajaq across the big bay. The
trip was long, and he couldn't find anything to
eat. He did find the angakoq, though, on the
distant shore.

PANIK

The angakoq must've known what to do.

> (The couple go to the
> ANGAKOQ on the other side
> of the stage.)

ANAANA

Oh yes, she did. She had great power on account
of being struck by lightning. She helped many
couples have babies. Anyway, the man came to
her, and she listened. Then she held out two
dried fish.

(ANGAKOQ retrieves the fish
from nearby.)

If you want a boy child, she said, give your
wife this fish. And if you want a girl child,
give your wife this fish.

PANIK

He must have jumped back into his qajaq and set
off right away.

ANAANA

Mmhmm. Off he went, paddling as fast as he
could, but it was a long way, and he was
awfully hungry.

(MAN paddles with evident
hunger.)

PANIK

Oh no. He didn't...

ANAANA

... He sure did! He had another day's journey,
yet, and still no sign of food.

(MAN weighs the fish in
hand, eating the girl fish
on ANAANA's cue.)

So he took a fish in either hand and weighed them, and decided it wouldn't be so bad if he ate just one. After all, he didn't need two babies, right now. One was enough. After a bit of thought, he decided he'd rather have a boy, so he put the boy fish away and ate the girl fish.

                    PANIK

I know what happens next. He gets a big belly, doesn't he?

                    ANAANA

First, he felt a cramp...

          (MAN responds sickly.)

... and then he felt awfully sick, but it wasn't seasickness. The water was calm. He didn't throw up, but it was a close call. He paddled home in record time.

          (PANIK laughs as the
          imagined MAN emerges with a
          giant belly.)

                    ANAANA

By the time he got home, his belly grew so big, he was wedged into his qajaq good and tight. His wife had to grease him up to pull him out of the qajaq. And once he was out, he had to waddle. His belly was huge!

                    PANIK

His wife must have been awfully surprised.

ANAANA

Yes, but she knew he was going to have a baby, so she knew how to take care of him.

>(WOMAN enters to care for MAN until the birth. She performs the action of ANAANA's story.)

She cared for him day and night, and one day, a baby passed from him, sliding out like a fish, plopping out into the cold air, caught in her hands. The couple loved their little girl very much. What did it matter if the man was an anaana, too?

PANIK

Wait——You're not saying that ataata is my real anaana, are you?

ANAANA

Maybe he is. Maybe he's not. I won't say. Either way, we love you, aakuluk.

>(lights dim on the GROUP onstage)

PANIK

Tell me a funny story, anaana.

ANAANA

What. That one wasn't funny enough for you?

PANIK

It was funny, but I want us both to laugh. Do you know the one about the giant who loved humans?

ANAANA

No, I don't think I know that one.

PANIK

It's a good one. There once was a giant.

> (The GREEN GIANT enters
> onstage, smacking his mouth
> with thirst. He goes to
> stand on a tall platform,
> motioning the actions of
> the story.)

He was huge and green. He was so big, that when
he was thirsty, he drained entire lakes. And
when he farted—huge windstorms!

ANAANA

That is big!

PANIK

He was married to another giant.

> (GIANTESS enters onstage
> and joins him on the tall
> platform.)

She was just as big as him, and just as green,
but he really liked us Inuits better than
giants. He thought we looked much better, being
so cute and tiny. He and his wife lived close
to an Inuit village, and he was friends with an
Inuk there.

> (MAN and WOMAN enter
> onstage, also motioning the
> actions of PANIK's story.)

That man had a beautiful wife with lots of
tattoos, and the giant watched her every day,
falling more and more in love with her. One
day, he asked the man if he'd be interested in
swapping wives, just for one night. The man
said he didn't mind, but would ask his wife
what she thought of it.

                    ANAANA

She couldn't have wanted to.

                    PANIK

You'd think, but she was prettier than she was
smart, so it didn't take long for her to be
convinced it might be fun.

                    ANAANA

Oh no.

                    PANIK

Oh yes. Although the man hadn't really thought
of it before the giant planted the suggestion
in his mind, now he just couldn't stop thinking
about the giantess, and her huge green vulva.

              (MAN daydreams, visibly
              intrigued. Then he leads
              the giant woman behind a
              masking wall to veil their
              erotic actions.)

He imagined bathing in that deep warm pool, and
off he went. He dove right in, but got sucked up
inside and was never seen again.

                    ANAANA

And the woman?

93

                    PANIK

She didn't do any better. The giant took her in
his hand, as gently as he could, and gazed at
her in adoration.

              (GREEN GIANT leads WOMAN to
              the opposite side of the
              stage behind a masking wall
              veiled to the audience.)

When he sighed, her hair blasted back from her
face. But no matter how gentle and kind the
giant tried to be, the end result was not good.
She was split right in half.

                    ANAANA

Augh!

                    PANIK

But it wasn't all bad. It made the giants
realize just how perfect they were for one
another, and when they kissed afterwards, the
ice floes cracked. And when they rolled together
naked, the whole ground shook.

                    ANAANA

              (laughs)

After a story like that, I know more than ever
that it is time for you to put your doll away.

                    PANIK

Just one more story, anaana?

ANAANA

Very well. One more. Did I tell you the one about the boy who carried fish home in his stomach?

>   (BOY enters with bulging
>   belly with AANAA trailing
>   behind.)

PANIK

In his stomach?

ANAANA

Yes. Listen. This boy wanted to be a brave one. A hunter. He lived with his aanaa, and one day, when the weather was calm, she asked him to walk along the beach to catch some fish. And so he began to walk in the shallows.

>   (BOY walks along the
>   imagined beach fishing,
>   bringing ANAANA's
>   storytelling to life.)

He had gone quite a long way when he saw a tommy cod. He darted his hands into the water and grabbed the fish. It was so slippery he was afraid he'd drop it, but he had nothing to hold it in. So he just opened his mouth and swallowed the whole fish. He felt it moving around in his throat, then swimming in his stomach.

PANIK

It was swimming inside of him? No!

95

ANAANA

>   (BOY wiggles with the
>   wiggling fish inside of him
>   and mimics the actions to
>   ANAANA's every word.)

But the tommy cod wasn't all he found. He found
a trout, a couple of white fish, and a big
salmon. All these he swallowed. Then he found a
narwhale, and he swallowed that, too.

PANIK

He did not swallow a narwhal. The tooth would
get stuck!

ANAANA

It wasn't easy. He had to wash it down with sea
water.

>   (BOY kneels as though to
>   lap from a body of water,
>   acting out ANAANA's words.)

And every time he swallowed something, it left
a ring of taste in the back of his throat. The
next thing he saw was a big, fat seal, but he
pulled its whiskers off before swallowing it.

PANIK

I suppose, those would get stuck in his throat.

ANAANA

Naturally. He found a beluga, and a walrus,
too. All of these he swallowed, and then he
decided he'd better get back home to his aanaa.

(BOY rises with bloated
stomach, drooping stomach
before walking backwards to
get caught in the rocks.)

His belly was huge and distended, by this time.
It was too big for him to walk. It drooped onto
the ground in front of him. He tried walking
backwards, but it dragged and kept getting
caught on rocks.

PANIK

What did he do?

(BOY resumes the action.)

ANAANA

Well, first he tried throwing it over his
shoulder like a sack, but that didn't go too
well. It was just too heavy and uncomfortable.
He stopped by a pond to get a drink, but with
the extra water, it just made everything in
his belly swim around even more, and now he
had bad cramps on top of everything else. He
hurt so badly, he was in tears. He managed to
get himself back to the shore, and dragged his
stomach out into the water until he floated and
bobbed in the waves. He kicked off with his
feet, and floated and bounced his way back to
his aanaa's skin tent.

PANIK

This isn't going to end well.

ANAANA

Oh, it does. His aanaa is astonished to see her
grandson floating back.

(AANAA exits from a tent,
working to drag BOY
into the tent, and when
unsuccessful she performs
the magic suggested by
ANAANA's words.)

And she tries to drag him into the skin tent,
but his stomach is just too big to get through
the door. Fortunately, the aanaa knew magic,
and she sat him beside a fire until a spark flew
out and landed on his stomach. The skin of his
belly was stretched so thin that the spark
burned right through, and all the fish came
slithering out in a big gurgle.

(BOY releases an abundance
of fish from his belly as
AANAA stitches his stomach
closed.)

And there they sat, surrounded by enough food
to last them for the entire winter. Aanaa
stitched his stomach closed again with caribou
sinew, and declared him a brave one.

(Lights dim on stage for
the imagined characters,
remaining on PANIK and
ANAANA.)

PANIK

Yes, he was a brave one. A grownup. You're
right, anaana.

ANAANA

About what?

PANIK

I'm a grownup, too. I sewed all the clothes for
my doll. (motions) I used stitches finer and
smaller than I'll ever have to do for my own
clothes. Though the doll has no arms, I used
the skin of ground squirrels' forelegs to make
sleeves. I'll never need to sew anything so
small again.

ANAANA

No, you won't. You'll have bigger things to
make.

PANIK

I checked everything I made twice. Three times.
I crimped the mukluks with my teeth. I wasted
no leather. Poor sewing means death. I sewed
well, didn't I, anaana?

ANAANA

You did. And now Sun Woman smiles upon you.

PANIK

(She sets aside her doll.)

I'm ready for my first tattoo.

(ANAANA and PANIK throat
sing together until one of
them loses the pattern and
then they laugh.)

Shantell Powell

Shantell Powell describes herself as a "two-spirit author, artist, and swamp hag of mixed Inuk/ Mi'kmaw/European ancestry." She lives in Ontario, Canada, and spends most of her time reading and writing. In the past, Powell has been a professional dancer, competitive athlete, martial artist, jeweler and costumer, comic shop manager, radio/club DJ, fashion/art model, botanical illustrator, and aerialist.

To elaborate on her eclectic life, she told Kinsman Quarterly, "I've sung in operas, acted in stage productions, and slept in a tent surrounded by wild elephants."

Her play, "A Time for Dolls," is a fun onstage piece showcasing Inuit storytelling. Inuit have a longstanding oral tradition, much of which is referred to today as Inuit mythology.

Powell reported that the Inuit are a circumpolar Indigenous people who live in northern lands claimed by Canada, the United States, Denmark, and Russia. Their traditional territories are some of the most inhospitable parts of the world; the survival of the people is a testament to their resilience. The Inuit traditional practices were made illegal during colonization, but these practices, such as kakiniit (Inuit tattooing), are experiencing a "renaissance."

"A Time for Dolls," Powell said, "is the coming-of-age story of an Inuk on the cusp of womanhood. It's a charming tale about sewing, fishing, survival cannibalism, spouse-swapping, and how people first learned to shit and give birth."

When asked about her inspiration for the play, Powell shared that she participated in a playwriting event where playwrights had 24 hours to write a new play in an unsettling environment. She wrote the first draft inside a dark warehouse filled with creepy sounds.

"I'd been reading up on Inuit folktales before the event and decided to showcase a few of them. I figured the framing narrative of a mother talking to her daughter would be a good way of presenting the stories."

Powell seemed elated to share the uniqueness of Inuit culture, but she also seemed compelled to discuss the atrocities of colonization that impacted the Indigenous community.

"In Canada, Inuit were forcibly relocated to desolate areas they'd never been to before as a way of staking territory for geopolitical reasons."

According to Powell, the RCMP (the Royal Canadian Mounted Police) slaughtered dog teams to contain Inuit to certain areas; children were kidnapped by the government and put in concentration/ re-education camps (residential schools), and some children were sold to white people to raise during the "60s scoop," which was the forced removal of Indigenous children from their families to foster homes between 1965 and 1984.

"To this day, children are still removed from Inuit families and placed in dangerous foster homes where they are raised for profit," Powell explained.

Powell also addressed the portrayal of Inuit as savages by the media, the pollution of Inuit territory, and the disregard for their traditions and beliefs. As for Powell herself, she works to uphold Inuit culture in her work and legacy.

"I want to share a cross-sampling of the rich and earthy stories of the Inuit," Powell said. "Inuit are a modern people with an ancient culture, and their creations are wonderful."

Africa

Section

3

The Wretchedness of the Earth
Joseph Marcel Ikhenoba

The Green Corn Dance

I stand on the foothills of Moccasin Mount

across the Lake Okeechobee

with my golden horn of fire and water

to whisper the haunting rhythm of drums.

Come, Soul Brother, take off that soggy soil

from beneath your shoes, stockings, and hues.

Open your nose, breathe the air

of our ancestral spirit, the Great Breath Maker

that sojourns through the eight walls of the clans

to purify the hollow day of the new dawn.

Joseph Marcel Ikhenoba

 Stomp and thump, sing and drink

with high spirits, to the Sun.

And lay our green corn tassels

before the moon and stars.

But first, Soul Brothers,

let's give Mother Nature our first green

of our cornflower, our early leaf

before dawn goes down to lay.

She has watered us from the nursery

in her long shower of rain

even when the scorching sun makes hail

under the roots of the bald cypress tree.

Wear your shirt and blouse.

Wear your shell shakers of turtle boxes

and dance around the sacred fire

of the four ancestral spirits of the clan.

Let the earth feel your stomping sole.

Let it resonate amidst your pumping soul.

Don't forget to pay homage

to the alligators, turtles, birds, and other creatures.

Purify your cold hands over a common grave.

Pass the green threshold over the village mound.

Though few may have crumpled the rose in your hair,

the river between is too short, and we will all kiss the soil.

Watch your anvil of burning coals.

Watch the odorous twilight of purple folds

that wraps the flames above the midnight knight

and dust the window panes of glimmering light.

Summon the lambs, parrots, deer, turtles, and alligators

to the dance, to the rhythm, to the blues.

Keep your hands open for the moon.

For there, the spirits of our ancestors ripple.

Joseph Marcel Ikhenoba

Sanctuary

Before you, the spirit of the eight clans
on those bent knees, limonite soil, I tremble.
Before your golden wreath, your sanctuary
I rustled my shadow on the floor—blown away.

I lie before your Moccasin roots
on the green corn stead of ancestral hues
under your cradle, a growing seedling
tender my roots for the sun to petiolate.

Out of the dust of the brown earth
crackle your divine tassels to my heart!
Creator of all, the Breath-Maker,
rekindle the fire of blossoming incense.

We kept hearing elegy
from among the lyre players
among lethargy.
Hearing the whirlwind across the shore
of fragments and discord among the knots.

Behind the crossroads of these burning trees,

the tangles of the scorching meadow,

we heard the buzzing of bees

stinging the dancers—

like they stung Osceola and

Billy Bowlegs.

We heard the vultures grunting on tree branches

to feast with shadows of their claws

and pick a corner on the wayside of the Everglades

in the water-logged trench of the Earth spirit.

Before you, the great spirit of the clan.

Listen to the chanting of our windpipes.

The white hyena wants to set falcons among the doves

and let the blood-dimmed ceremony drown.

Everywhere, the white dove nested,

it looked like a grave, with ethereal eyes and quietness.

But Elders of the eight clans,

help us not to lose our dance and our folktale songs.

Joseph Marcel Ikhenoba

Son Of Fire

They say I am a sojourner, a castaway.

The wind blew my ancestors to Florida marsh.

At the death of night, a whispering tide

to feed on squashes and wild meat.

They say I am a leech on a beach

cut away from its shell,

swerving in the mist, basking in the sun.

But the river knows its source.

I am the Son of Fire

with a store of Vermeil roses at a meadow,

bright and free like the sea,

but don't touch a scorpion's tail.

I am the river whose mouth dunes.

The white hyena pours his chemicals.

But I am rock, a crust of steel.

A bow of fire

Joseph Marcel Ikhenoba

Joseph Marcel Ikhenoba, published author and poet, holds a B.Sc. and M.Sc. in Biochemistry from the University of Nigeria, Nsukka, and the University of Lagos, Akoka. He is one of the finalists for Kinsman Quarterly's Native Voices Award, representing the Bini tribe of Edo State, Nigeria.

The Bini Tribe is one of the oldest and most influential cultures in Nigeria. The people practice a traditional religion centered on ancestor worship and a pantheon of deities, not unlike the Indigenous groups from the Americas. In fact, in Ikhenoba's collection, "The Wretchedness of the Earth," he channels the challenges of his own culture to reflect the challenges of the American Indigenous.

"The maltreatment of the Indigenous Americans, especially the Seminole tribe of Alabama and Georgia, and how the United States government evicted their forefathers from their native lands through wars, injustice, and torture to the swampy Everglades in Florida inspired the narrative," Ikhenoba said. "It was the highest height of injustice. But the Seminoles adapted and continued their festivals, such as the Green Corn Festival and summoning of ancestral spirits."

"The Green Corn Dance," "Sanctuary," and "Son of Fire" are the lineup in the poet's series, each marking the power of ancestral influence within the earth, not unlike the traditions of Ikhenoba's own Bini culture.

"The historical story still resonates today in Africa and especially in the Bini kingdom, whose destroyed lands, artifacts, and exiled king by the British government played a huge role in redefining its history. But today, the kingdom still stands in its ruins," said Ikhenoba. "This isn't to create an ambience of apathy towards the British or the people of the United States, but to allow us to learn from history the shortfalls of power when imposed on other cultures and traditions."

Besides his prolific writing life, Ikhenoba enjoys volunteer work in the community, along with sports, research, traveling, and cooking. He has multiple publications, including "Weathering World" (2020) and "Remember," published by Poetry South Journal. His short stories, "The Murder" and "Abeokuta Women Protest," were published by Writers Space Africa. More of Ikhenoba's collections will be featured in the upcoming *Iridescence* anthology published by Kinsman Avenue Publishing, Inc.

A Defiled Manhood
Sunday Abel

A man who defiles his manhood commits an unpardonable offence, but denying the misuse challenges the wit and sacredness of the deities of the land, the inviolable adjudicator.

Desmond gripped the scaly legs of the hen. Both he and his accuser hand-carried their birds as was the procedure for such an occasion. The Akpu-abada deity wouldn't accept a cock, for cocks lacked resilience.

Desmond's eyes rose and settled on the crown of the Anunube tree. In Igbo land, the Anunube was the incarnation of the gods. Everything said about the ageless tree was true, its long-standing dreadfulness and tranquility. They said it was as old as the village and as mysterious as a lake.

Most of the shrines in Igbo land had this type of tree. It towered over the others, sinewy in its ferociousness, unshapely, gigantic, and intimidating. Any bird that perched on its branches died quietly on the spot. No human came close and survived the night, except on the chief priest's instruction and consent.

113

It was said that the gods took refuge in the Anunube. No tree grew near it; any that came in contact with it, withered outright. It was as fearsome as it was reputable for its usefulness. The tree healed all manners of ailments if consumed according to the priest's prescription. Juju was made from the tree to enchant people, a talisman for protection and good luck as it housed the deity.

To utter a lie before Akpu-abada was to choose to die an undignified death, to permit oneself to be thrown like an Ebola victim down the steep of Akpu-abada Mountain without a tearful farewell from loved ones. Whoever this deity killed, died unusually, without quaking, the body turned white within minutes of the last breath. This omen was the indication that the god was responsible for the victim's demise.

Desmond accepted this fate. He would lie about misusing his manhood before the great Akpu-abada. In Imeoha, as well as surrounding villages, to misuse one's manhood was rare and to misstate before Akpu-abada was suicidal. But not all who lied died, yet calamity came as certain as the rising and setting sun.

Once a woman, the seventh wife of a chief, grew dissatisfied with the once-a-week sex ration from her husband. She sought a younger man from a nearby village and kept their affair secret. The husband discovered it, and a case came before the ancestral adjudicator. The wife denied the affair before the deity, saying she never opened her legs for another man. Unsurprisingly, Akpu-abada killed her accuser's hen, and she left disgracefully with hers alive.

Afterwards, everyone waited for her death in the few days following the conviction. She didn't die. Instead, her life went wrong, becoming proverbial, always on the lips of the elders when morality lessons and speeches on fidelity were given to the younger generation.

The woman's life became miserable. She opened her legs for everyone. Men—young and old—climbed on top of her in private and public. Whoever wanted relief from their libido sought her out and found it. But those who did shared in her curse, dying before their time in unacceptable ways. Some slipped from palm trees, falling to their death. Others died on top of their wives, by the side of the road, or disgracefully with protruded bellies.

Desmond's eyes fell upon the grotesque masque of the deity whose voice must be strictly followed. He doubted the masque could prove his guilt and was rather excited to see if any phenomenon might take place. Had he committed any other crime other than the one he was accused of, he wouldn't have bothered to lie. But misusing his manhood was deemed heinous, even more so to have done it against a friend, the only one in Imeoha who understood his tongue. The one who told him the little he knew about the village and this deity.

Under Desmond's feet lay the decaying variegated feathers belonging to those whom the deity acquitted of the wrongdoing. Once the accuser and accused presented their case, the deity killed the bird of the innocent. It usually died peacefully, not from strangling, slashing of the neck, or smashing. It died bloodlessly from the spoken words of the chief priest without any torrential quake in its last breath.

Desmond Afamuefuna arrived in the Imeoha village only a few weeks ago from Massachusetts, where his Nigerian parents naturalized. His father told him he was old enough to get to know the area of his roots. Desmond only understood the White Man's English, speaking through his nose as the villagers would say. He spoke in a "ya men, ya men" fashion that was unacceptable. A true son of the soil spoke the language of his ancestors; he followed the culture and traditions of his native land. Desmond planned to spend the summer achieving these things, but then he misused his manhood, causing him to appear before the dreaded Akpu-abada.

In Massachusetts, it was impossible to misuse one's manhood. Everybody used their manhood however it pleased them. Once his college friend caught him staring at the sprouting hair around the shaft of his pelvis. Desmond was pleased with those hairs and took every opportunity to go into the toilet to see if they were still growing. That older friend caught him and taught him how to use his manhood in the way Desmond would later try in his ancestral home.

The accuser, Thomas, was a boy whose head attached to his body by a string of a neck that swung this way and that as he walked. Such a slender neck was not enough for the head but well suited for his pendulous legs. The collarbone rose from his shoulder blades and fell into his body on the lower base of his neck. His eyes were a dense black, and his countenance showed his feelings of betrayal.

Thomas's name had been given to him when he joined a newly planted protestant church, the first of many in Imeoha. During his baptism, Thomas doubted if ordinary water was capable of washing away his many sins. When the priest told him that baptism was symbolic, Thomas pleaded that he be allowed to stay for days in the holy water where others had only been momentarily immersed. From that came about the name Thomas at the expense of his renounced Igbo name, Anyasi, meaning *darkness*.

Because of his new faith, he was forbidden to appear before Akpu-abada for litigation or to seek spiritual help from the deity. To do so was to acknowledge the supremacy of the god over his own. But Thomas wouldn't allow a crime such as misusing one's manhood to go unpunished. Doing so would result in his own death for not revealing the abominable offense.

He gazed at Desmond before returning his eyes to the chief priest who seemed ready to preside over the case.

The chief priest performed incantations in a tongue only understood between him and the deity, then he broke the kola nut and threw it against the terrifying masque. He poured libation on the ground for the sleeping ancestors to bear witness. Both the accused and accuser were given alligator pepper to clear their voices and purge their lips of evil, making them audible to the gods.

Desmond chewed his alligator pepper and swallowed with pride. Then he contemptuously pointed a *fuck-you* finger at his accuser, who grimaced as if to say *you shall see.*

Previous cases in Imeoha included allegations of a wife killing her husband. A man claims possession of a late brother to the detriment of his widow and children; quarrels over land ownership or theft. There had never been a case of one misusing one's manhood, and thus, the stage was set for the gods without precedence.

"Anyasi," the chief priest called, peering at Thomas. He wouldn't call him by his protestant name for only Igbo and the languages between the priest and deity were allowed. The chief priest frenetically shook his head, poised to speak the deity's message to the litigants.

"Hold this *ofor.*" He handed Thomas a woebegone stick with too many joints for its length.

"Speak nothing but the truth to Akpu-abada who already knows the truth." He paused and peeked at the masque. The white feathers looped in a creaky white cloth fastened around the Anunube tree along with the blood-smeared cloth knitted with limpets, snail, and tortoise shells. Every space was occupied by calabashes of different sizes and skulls of various animals. An evil spirit seemed to hover over them; a haunting eeriness that gave the shrine its deserved frightfulness.

The chief priest was an old man who wore a thick copse of white hair surrounding the bald patch on his head. His face was decorated with native chalk, and a long gray beard and moustache curled over his mouth. He whistled and extolled the deity in the unknown language while Desmond appeared lost in the labyrinth charade of justice.

"To lie before Akpu-abada is to challenge a hungry lion to a fight, the beginning of the end of whoever does it. *Nwata na agba egwu suru gede, omakwa na surugede bu egwu ndi nmou? Ukpana okpoko gburu, bu kwa nu nti chiri ya.*"

117

The youths waited outside the shrine, punctuating the flow of the proceedings with boisterous singing. An exaltation overflowed from the spectators aggrieved that their land had been sullied by Desmond. Leaves, slabs, and stems rose and fell to commensurate the crime committed. The villagers awaited judgement.

The historic feats of Akpu-abada were still fresh in their hearts. The elders who stood among them jerked their fists and wagged their walking-sticks. The infuriated tore off their chieftain caps. Desmond's offense could unleash the gods' wrath against Imeoha. It could bring strange illnesses upon the people, cause locusts and beetles to devour the crops, or force the Avuna stream, the only source of water, to dry up. The land must be cleansed from Desmond's abominable deed, so the elders came to prosecute him as well as determine how best to avert the impending wrath.

Thomas raised the *offor* to his mouth, gobbled down his collected spittle, and cleared his throat to speak.

"I have come not to seek justice for my own sake but for the sake of our land. I will speak nothing but the truth. Should I say an untrue thing before the great Akpu-abada, may my life go wrong." He paused and eyed Desmond, who seemed unperturbed. "When he arrived in this village, my master Reverend Joseph told me to show him 'round the village. Afterwards, we ate from the same plate and slept in the same bed, sometimes in his father's house, sometimes in the priest's. Yesterday, while we slept in his father's house in the same bed in the middle of the night, he did that which is unspeakable." Thomas stammered, glancing at Desmond and the chief priest who urged him to continue.

"I was jolted from sleep by a stick-like object, intruding into my anus. It was powerful and painful. I pushed away whatever it was from my body. On a closer look, it was him—Desmond with his stiff organ in his hands. That's why we have appeared before you," he concluded with a sigh of relief.

"Aru!" interjected the chief priest. The *offor* was handed to Desmond to state his defense.

Desmond arrogantly collected the rusty stick from Thomas but did so with his left hand. The chief priest rebuked him for being uncivil as it was forbidden for left hands to give or receive items within the vicinity of Akpu-abada. Even the left-handed used their right hands within the shrine, an unwritten code that Thomas had previously warned Desmond about, but Desmond sought to taunt the chief priest.

He returned the stick to Thomas, recollecting it with his right hand. Desmond raised the *offor* to his mouth, then brought it down. He glowered scornfully at the chief priest and returned the *offor* to his mouth and spoke, "Fuck! You! Fuck you, motherfucker."

"Aru!" Thomas exclaimed, holding his hen tightly with his right hand, the other covering his mouth. The chief priest was oblivious.

Desmond stooped and then hastily straightened up. He twirled the hen in his hand while in a pirouette, much to the consternation of the onlookers. Desmond then struck the hen against the Anunube tree and bolted out of the shrine. The hen quaked and died.

Sunday Abel

Sunday Abel is a journalist and writer of Nigeria whose literary works have earned several prizes, including the Creator of Justice Literary Awards by the International Human Rights Art Festival Movement, New York. His riveting short story, "A Defiled Manhood," confronts the collision of an American-Nigerian with the culture of his parents' homeland.

Abel is among the finalists of the Native Voices Award and is of the Igbo people group. The Igbo people are among the largest ethnic groups in Nigeria, primarily located in the southeastern part of the country. They have a rich cultural heritage and a diverse set of traditions that have been preserved over centuries.

The Igbo society is organized around the extended family, which includes not only parents and children but also grandparents, aunts, uncles, cousins, and other relatives. The family is the primary social unit.

As illustrated in "A Defiled Manhood," traditional religious practices of the Igbo involve ancestral deities, masks, and ritual performances. In Abel's profound story, he discusses the authority of the Akpu-abada deity, which holds the power to impose justice within the community through supernatural powers.

Abel's character, Desmond, epitomizes the Western arrogance and disconnect from Igbo traditions. The story even alludes to the perverted violation of Western culture upon cultural beliefs.

The expression of parables and proverbs is greatly valued in Igbo communication, often used to convey cultural values. Throughout Abel's short story, he does a powerful job of recapturing the traditional values and beliefs of Igbo culture, showing its overall significance and power.

Sunday Abel

Desert Pearl and Other Poems
Tonnie MAC

Desert Pearl

Through the milk-white, innocent eyes
popping to stand the test of time,
surrounded by wobbly tired gait of maturity,
all sung in choir with approval of a savior born—
a stone they desired to polish to a diamond
and dazzle the dully valley of doom.

At a tender age he knew the burden he'd carry
and wasted no time to fit the shoes.
Science, art, and languages fit the tiny brain.
Bravery would mend the dire delirium at home.

Tonnie MAC

Rout and rogue were never a cup to drink from.

To fail father was a fate to dread.

His radiance outshone the stars,

prompting his father to call the realtor.

Fertile soil and woolly sheep, nothing to curt the spark.

With a proud pledge he'd say, "My son, my gem,

for your shield of knowledge,

mounts I'd level for a dime."

He'd trade the harvest's bounty,

for wisdom's single seed,

forsaking a treat of meat and feta cheese.

With zeal he aced the tests with skill,

as kin flocked in plenty to merry,

while dean conferred honors so high,

he'd wield the sword of words and wisdom.

Father's golden sun. He'd light the dark slum.

He vowed and strove to shine the pearl for all.

Suited up, he hit the road to get cracking.

One said, "overqualified." Another, "a novice."

Next craved a lusty favor and a ransom out of measure.

Facing a wall of cruelty, he sailed a storm of scorn and sleaze,

and braved the bribe, the bait, the blow.

With pearl, cracked, corroded, faded, the rich fill their nests.

Oh People! You've spurned a gem and

flung it into a desert of dismay.

You've stained it with your shams and chained with cruel sway.

Once an ocean of love and care, now a desert of phantom dreams.

Moisten your pearl with trust.

Let the stream of life soothe their fray.

Wake up, People, see the pearl you recklessly lost.

Let him shine bright. Like a fane, the bleak slum will rave.

Bright Light. Dim Light. DARK.

In the midst of the raging waves,

they watched her gulp the callous cunning darts.

Her crumbly heart cruelly impaled; the fate that enslaves.

So fondly she'd mask the marks.

Her soul would ache and bleed from life's glaives.

She cried an ocean for redemption from a life perpetually stark.

In desperation, the rope ends it.

With stigma the chums looked in utter scorn,

and nattered her solitary life she so drowned in.

As a jest they'd laugh it off and know not the pain borne.

Options to content would be the faster poison to kick in.

The jeer and tough love, be strong. Would suicide suborn?

Yet blithely a random word alienates, even with the kin.

The loop finally tightens round the neck.

With croc tears the mates flock to condole.

"If this message would reach Mary in heaven;

life lost so young—" all will strive to console.

For what? She writhed in pain and longed for a haven,

but scornfully, her soul you shunned like a rotten pole.

Her tombstone, now a patch-spot for a raven.

World's cold shoulders soaked in her silent tears.

Be chaste, fair-weather friend, lest you atone.

Religion and priests you've scorned,

while the vain fanes of pretense you adorn.

In exalted hallow worship, you plead with Him

to remold the hearts of clay to vessels of honor.

Yet in your hearts of tin you curse and vilify—

you thought it was an act and left her marooned.

For remaining Mary, my soul cries to you.

Blinded by constant flopped success.

For the media, it'd hurt not to leave a cue.

Live the sacred life, gifted as a princess.

And flout their nonsensical bleats of an ewe.

I'll wait on the podium for a fess.

It's never the end—you'll ever chew the bitter pill.

Perfect Son

Dare bite that pie, and I will your head.

You've disgraced the family—I bear the shame.

Young in age, yet frail in resolve.

Full of energy, but lacking in wisdom.

No spouse, no children, 35 and still counting...

A sweet couch potato, I spit on your face.

Why can't you be like the neighbor's son?

Oh, Father! I can't bear the pressure anymore.

I detest the torment, for you demand the unattainable.

If not for the family resemblance, I'd doubt my lineage.

For you have turned my life into torment—my soul finds no peace.

We play cat and mouse as resentment eats away at me.

When will you understand—

I am not the neighbor's son.

Sadly! I have a mule for a son!

What a parliament my house has become.

Obstinacy runs in the veins, definitely not from me.

A cold you caught—maybe? Where's your meekness?

I loathe your tenacity; it hurts like a sting.

I pray diligence locates you.

If only you'd emulate the neighbor's son!

Forgive me for not showing due respect.

Pardon my defiance yet again.

It's never my intention, for my world is cruel.

Yesterday you witnessed my fiancée's contempt

for I couldn't get her the fog,

despite the allergies, I got the boot.

For a damned soul, even cold beer will burn.

Relax son, the world won't absolve; it's a judge with no mercy.

Beware boy, even at worst, frost shall still bite.

Grow your anchors strong, and tides shall not wash you.

Rise above the whining, and the sun will favor your talents.

Grumbling won't fill your belly.

Embrace the strength of a lion I was—and roar.

And the neighbor's son will admire your bravery.

With attention, I heed your counsel.

I share your blood, but not the drive.

I walk not your path. I remain inimitable.

I admire your feats, but they bear your signature.

Tonnie MAC

I am unique and support my course.

To succeed, I am eager to accomplish.

For I am neither you nor the neighbor's son.

Excuse the gall, my son, you're an unpolished gem.

With expectancies, I crushed your spirit.

With delayed success, I burned with rage.

To uphold family honor, I lost my son.

Guide me, son. Teach me to walk your path.

I will call the producer and pay for the record.

You are my boy, not the neighbor's son.

I get a hundred a day, but your care's a grand.

The most tender songs of admiration.

The best I have is "the dad I love."

The best I possess is the father I cherish.

Your care shall not only bear promises,

but sail to the top I'll broadly cast.

For I am not the neighbor's son.

Tonnie MAC

Tonnie MAC, born Anthony Mutunga Charles, is a native of Kenya. His poetry collection "Desert Pearl and Other Poems" represents the diverse cultural heritage of his home country, drawing inspiration from the collective experiences of its people. According to MAC, the poems represent the life of a Kenyan.

"It is like a reflection of what everyone passes through, especially the youth," the poet said.

MAC described his native land as "a cradle of humanity," a nation that is rich in cultural heritage and traditions.

"It's a land where storytelling, dance, and art are not just forms of entertainment but vital instruments of a rich heritage that shape our society," MAC told Kinsman Quarterly. "The beliefs are as varied as the landscapes, from the snow-capped peaks of Mount Kenya to the sun-soaked shores of the Indian Ocean. And some arid and semi-arid regions of Eastern and Northeastern Kenya."

According to MAC, the social interactions of Kenya "are imbued with a religious norm of life."

"Children grow up and become the salvation of the old generations. Parents raise their children with high hopes, sometimes imposing their past failures on the shoulders of the children to rectify them," MAC said. "If a parent had a dream of becoming a doctor or a musician, they believe that they failed because they did not have enough resources. They would, in turn, invest heavily in their sons or daughters to become the doctors that they did not become. So, youths grow up with a lot of expectations on their backs."

MAC's collection is a reflection of resilience amidst adversity, "a beacon of hope in the face of despair." The poet insisted that the collection is a call to recognize the inherent strength within each individual. The poems explore themes of identity, societal expectations, and the transformative power of self-belief.

"The overarching message is one of empowerment and the enduring spirit of humanity. It's a reminder that within each of us lies a 'Pearl,' the potential to shine even in the harshest conditions, and that we should be conscious of the pearls around us."

MAC plans to continue to use poetry as a vessel for change, to inspire and empower, and to leave a legacy that uplifts the voices of his community.

Beyond poetry, MAC is passionate about social entrepreneurship, climate action, and youth empowerment. He runs a company, called Green-Core Energy Limited, reflecting his dedication to his interests.

When sharing about Kenyans as a people group, MAC affirmed with pride, "We are a testament to the power of hope and the relentless pursuit of a better tomorrow."

Every First June
Sophia Obianamma Ofuokwu

Every first of June, you have the same dream. A man in a spinning car waves at you. You never wave back. He looks familiar in a dress shirt that billows around him as his car spins off the road. His eyes beg you to remember, but all you know is that you have had this dream from your beginning. You never bothered your mother about it. She had a lot to deal with your father.

He had always been a strange fixture in the house—your father. Loud on drunk evenings. Brooding when the money was long coming.

People say their father's money belongs to them. You never enjoyed his. You only knew he has been paid when he comes home chattering about Imabong, the bar girl, reeking of perfume and booze. He would complain of being broke in the middle of the month, so you knew he had given his money to Imabong.

You have slept in this house all your life because the educational institutions you attended are a trekkable distance. Staying in a school environment had its perks and disadvantages.

A perk granted you entry into parties and hangouts with cool university students. These, unlike your mates at your technical college, lived in a constant state of energy and daredevilry. A disadvantage was that everyone knows you as the daughter of Imabong's lover.

You have seen her. A pale girl who used her fair share of creams and struggled with skin that revolts the chemicals. You would feel pity for her if she was not a cancer eating into your home. Admittedly, a sub-functional abode, but a home nonetheless.

On the 29th of May 2023, your father returned home drunk and angry. Imabong was in some other man's arms. As usual, you bore the brunt of his anger. He spat the usual curse: attacks on your femininity, your large bust, your inclination to join the University students at the bar.

It happened when you tried to placate him with "Daddy, calm down *na*."

You shouldn't tell an angry person to calm down—especially a proud Yoruba man like your father. You should know that by now.

You should have made sure that when you did tell a person to calm down, it was not the man who was not your father. Because as inebriated as he was, he could have turned your life upside down, inviting a barrage of questions that would unwind your very existence.

"Don't call me daddy, useless whore! Find your father in the dirty grave your witch of a mother sent him to. You two will not kill me like you killed the man! And they warned me about you *Akwa-ibom* people *o!*"

You noticed the irony in his statement and wondered where he thinks *Imabong* was from. You would have given him three guesses.

When he walked out of your life on the epiphany that your mother, who was standing still at the kitchen door, might concoct a poison to end his life, you did not feel the loss. Wasn't he always a stranger?

Your mother was no stranger, though, was she? It was all a joke. A horrible gut-wrenching joke, but a joke still. She wouldn't have lied to you for 24 years with a smile that spoke of openness and trust. She would have never hidden your identity from you so wickedly. *She would never.*

Yes, she was no stranger. No stranger indeed because her confession came as the questions appeared in your eyes. She knew to keep her distance. To be as succinct as possible through the snot and the tears. She knew to bring evidence and all the information you'd need while your mind was still forming questions.

No, she was no stranger. But didn't they say something about the betrayal of family?

It hurts.

You were not Yoruba. That was the first dagger to your heart. You were not of the tribe you have worn proudly, like your favourite *aso-oke*.

It stung as much as the realization that you had not dreamt your father's arms caressing you when you were twelve. You could accept now what he accepted when he did that to you. That you were not blood. You were from *Akwa-ibom*, you were *Anaang*, but you knew nothing about them except for the fact that your mother was one, and she had family somewhere there.

"Why?" This was the culmination of your perplexity.

"I was stingy. With his memory."

"It should have been mine too!"

Her words were slow but hit you with the determination of 24 years of lies.

"You didn't know him!"

"So, you hoard his memory? The way you hoard everything you are ashamed of? The way you hoard the actual reason your boss pays you thrice what you should earn?"

When she fell to the ground, you wondered if she would ever forgive you. For knowing. For accepting that your mother did what some helpless women with deadbeat husbands and a daughter to raise did.

You wondered too, as you left the house, if you could ever forgive her. You returned in three days and ignored the sounds of her grief. The kitchen was never loud before 5:30 p.m. You fleetingly wondered what her boss must have thought of the absence. You also wondered if he was called father by another man's child.

How would it have happened? Like in your case?

Did the actual father die prior to his child's birth? Did the grieving mother marry him while another man's child was in her womb so the child would never lack a father's love? Of course, such a case was peculiar to you, but you could not help it. You wanted someone else to be as confused as you were. How to be? How to be?

You fell asleep with your father's picture in your arms. This man whose blood ran through your veins. You wanted to see him tonight.

The trailer up ahead blared its horn. The driver just discovered his brake was faulty. The man in the Volvo raised his head at the sudden sound. And in the only functioning headlight of the truck going the wrong way and too fast for a man parked on the side of the road to consider escaping, he saw his life flash before his eyes.

He saw himself wave at a daughter he had not yet met. A smile broke out on his face when you finally waved back. The collision made your body twitch, but even as the world spun, you smiled.

You remembered now. Who you were. Even if only in the fleeting moments shared with a man long dead in the realm of dreams.

You remembered.

No, you were not the daughter of Imabong's lover.

From your bedroom door, your mother watched you smile. She offered a teary grin at the luminous figure outside the window as they watched their daughter learn about home.

It would be a long journey, but the promise of home was worth it.

Sophia Obianamma Ofuokwu

Sophia Obianamma Ofuokwu, Indigenous author of "Every First June," is a Nigerian student at the College of Nursing and Midwifery. She enjoys writing poetry and short stories and has been featured in several publications, including Kinsman Quarterly's "Black Diaspora" and "Native Voices" anthologies.

Ofuokwu's people group is of the Anioma region, which she describes as a community rooted in respect and love.

"I come from a people who are explorers. We proliferate, we move," she said. "If you look around you and see an Igbo person smiling back, understand that it is because we enjoy moving to new places and learning new things."

The writer shared about the unifying traditions that strengthen the culture of her community. "Festivals are very important to my people, as celebrations tend to be joyful and serve as avenues for coming together as one. One such festival is the Iwaji. The Iwaji is an annual yam festival still practiced, where we gather to celebrate the end of the harvest and show our gratitude to the deities for a fruitful year."

According to Ofuokwu, it is at festivals like this that the Anioma people return home to spend time with family and show collective appreciation for the success of the harvest season. The Anioma people are always eager to "break bread with kin."

When asked about her feelings on the Western influence upon her community, Ofuokwu discussed the good and bad of it.

"Firstly, with Western civilization comes Western innovations and culture, feminism, and the doing away with some harmful traditional practices. This is the good part," Ofuokwu admits. "With Western civilization, though, we also have the blotting of our own culture of brotherhood and the things that make us who we are, to create space for the new and shiny. Western civilization is a double-edged sword to my people."

The writer often explores themes of self-concept in her work. In "Every First June," the protagonist scrambles for identity after she is confronted with the news of her biological father.

"I wanted to write something about lost identity because I was battling with these issues myself," Ofuokwu explained. "That was all the story needed to write itself, really."

Ofuokwu aspires to use her writing to "encompass the human nature in all its gore and beauty," and succeed in bringing hope to everyone who reads her work.

Acknowledgments

As we conclude this anthology of Indigenous writers, we extend our heartfelt gratitude to all who have made this collection possible, including guest judge Tim Jones of the Seminole Tribe of Florida.

Special thanks go to our Co-Editors, Dawn Leas, Sandyha Barlaas, and Odette Cortés, whose unwavering dedication, insightful guidance, and collaborative spirit have been instrumental in shaping this anthology. Your hard work and commitment have been truly invaluable.

We also wish to express our deep appreciation to Anastasia Simone, whose brilliant cover design encapsulates the profound marriage between the natives and the earth. Your artistry has given our anthology a visual identity that speaks volumes.

A warm thank you to Summer Greigh for her tireless effort in designing the book's interior. Your attention to detail and aesthetic sensibilities have created a beautiful and inviting experience for our readers.

To Radiyah and Sophia, the contestants who began this journey as authors but became integral to the project itself, we thank you. Your investment, passion, and dedication have enriched this anthology beyond measure.

Lastly, I extend my deepest gratitude to my grandfathers, beautiful men of Indigenous heritage. While I wish they had passed down the glory of our native traditions, I am profoundly grateful for the native DNA they have bestowed upon me.

— Monique Franz

www.ingramcontent.com/pod-product-compliance
Lightning Source LLC
Chambersburg PA
CBHW070046260626
47159CB00005B/2134